C000132662

# LEARNING

# CURVE

## AN INSTALOVE AGE-GAP
## ROMANCE

## NICHOLE ROSE

Nichole Rose

Copyright © 2021 by Nichole Rose

All rights reserved. This book or any portion thereof may not be reproduced or used in any manner whatsoever without the express written permission of the author except for the use of brief quotations in a book review.

All characters appearing in this work are fictitious. Any resemblance to real persons, living or dead, is purely coincidental.

# CONTENTS

# DEDICATION

For Paige. Thanks for always being a willing participant in my bad ideas.

# About the Book

**Two wrongs make the best right for an over-the-top professor and curvy graduate student.**

### Maya Denver

My mom always said there are plenty of fish in the sea.

But she never met Kane Maxwell.

He's the only fish I see.

He's everything I've ever wanted in a man—caring, intelligent, hot, and bossy.

The only problem?

He has no clue who I am until I sign up for a curvy dating app and match with him.

He knows who I am now...except for that one pesky detail I forgot to mention.

He's my new professor.

And classes begin Monday.

## Kane Maxwell

Three days ago, I fell in love with an angel and did the unthinkable.

I joined the dating app I heard her talking about just so I could find her.

When I do, she's everything I knew she would be--beautiful, sweet, sassy.

Her big green eyes and voluptuous curves drive me wild.

The only problem?

Relationships with students are strictly forbidden.

I should have told her the truth from the start.

But when she looks at me, I'm not thinking about class.

All I'm thinking about is making her mine forever.

If you enjoy steamy age-gap romance, OTT protective older men, and an extra dose of sugary-sweet romance, you'll love Maya and Kane's story! As always, Nichole Rose books come with no cheating and a guaranteed HEA.

# CHAPTER ONE
## KANE

"I'm thinking about signing up for a dating app."

I sit forward in my chair, listening intently as the curvy bombshell on the other side of the privacy wall announces her news to her friends. They have no idea I'm listening, but I've been eavesdropping like a motherfucker since the hostess led them to a booth thirty minutes ago. It's rude and I'm going to hell, I know. Sue me.

But anyone else in my position would be doing the same. Since I'm eating alone like usual, their conversation is far more scintillating than anything happening at my booth. That's not why I'm eavesdropping, though.

Maya, the curvy raven-haired goddess with the incredible green eyes, is responsible for that. As soon as she walked in, my eyes were on her. She's maybe five-seven, with wildly curly hair, an almost impish smile, and curves for days. In short, she's a fucking knockout. She's soft-spoken, but she doesn't have to be loud to be heard. She weaves magic with her words and that sweet voice.

In the last thirty minutes, I've learned a lot about her. She was born and raised in Nashville, loves her job teaching elementary school, adores her students, is wickedly funny, and incredibly astute. She prefers beer to mixed drinks, loves music, and is a hockey fan. If I had a type, she'd check every box. I haven't even spoken to her, and I'm already hooked.

This is a problem.

I'm an associate law professor at Vanderbilt...and she's a graduate student. She let that little tidbit slip a few minutes ago. That should have deflated my dick quick, fast, and in a hurry. It didn't.

I can't remember the last time someone caught my interest like this. No. I take that back. I can remember. It's never happened. I'm thirty-nine, and my dating life is non-existent. Between teaching and running my family's law firm, what little free-time I have is devoted to more mundane tasks. Like eating, sleeping, exercising, or catching up on the list of shit my Ma needs done at her place.

I love my mother like crazy, but she's been renovating her monstrosity of a house since she bought it after my dad died two years ago. If she doesn't give it up soon, I'm going to lose my mind. Installing new dry wall is exactly as infuriating as it sounds. Rewiring the electricity and fixing the plumbing aren't much better. And fuck painting. Whoever invented paint was an asshole.

"What? Seriously?" Maya's blonde friend, Cassidy, says. "Please tell me it's not the one for farmers."

"No, of course not," Maya says with a crystalline laugh that makes my dick twitch. The greedy bastard has been standing at attention for the last half hour. "It's called *Curve Connection*. It was designed by curvy women for curvy women."

"Please tell me there aren't a bunch of pervs on it," Megan, her petite friend, says. "Because, seriously, if I get one more unsolicited dick pic from some random creep on the internet who thinks I'm desperate just because I'm a big girl, I'm rioting."

"We ride at dawn," Cassidy says in a sports-announcer voice.

All three of them crack up.

I smile, listening to them. Women are wild, and we love the shit out of them for it. But if they ever do riot, I'm taking their side. Doesn't even matter what they demand, I'm in. If there is a treasure in this world worth guarding, it's women. My dad taught me that. There is nothing he wouldn't have done for my Ma or my baby sister.

"Don't forget to watch out for the married men on dating sites," Megan says a moment later.

"And the ones who say they're looking for love but really only want to hook up," Cassidy adds.

"And the ones who decide you're not compatible for the most asinine reasons, and then try to mansplain why you're wrong about something they clearly know nothing about."

"Guys on the internet suck," Maya says, causing my smile to slip.

They're not wrong. I know exactly how fucked up men can be, especially when they're hiding behind a screen. It's a never-ending source of worry for me. My sister, Kenna, is twenty-four and independent as hell. She's also an aspiring musician. My blood boils when I see the shit men post on her videos. If I ever find any of them, may God have mercy on their souls. I sure as hell won't.

It pisses me off to think about Maya dealing with the same shit on this dating app. Actually, thinking about her dating anyone bugs me. I don't even know her, but I already feel...protective of her. The feeling has nothing to do with my job, either.

There's just something about her that makes me want to scoop her up in my arms and hold her close or beat my chest and roar that she's mine. There's a sadness lurking deep in her eyes that demands a response. It's some primal instinct that grows a little bit more demanding the longer I listen to her conversation. I want this girl in my bed where she belongs, not on some dating app meeting random assholes who won't appreciate her for the goddess she is.

*Then do something about it*, a little voice whispers.

Technically, dating her isn't against the rules. Classes don't resume until Monday, and from what I gather, she's working on her Master's in Education, not law. The only seminar I teach in that program is an educational law seminar for first year students. She's well into her second year. Pursuing a relationship with her wouldn't violate policy, but professor and student relationships are strongly frowned upon anyway. When Jared Kingston married Caroline Thorne a few years ago, people were scandalized.

The thing is though...I'm not sure I give a flying fuck about the rules or anyone's delicate sensibilities. What people think about me has never interested me much. In fact, I don't give two shits if people like me or not. Most of them grate on my fucking nerves. I teach because it's far easier to educate people about the law than it is to defend them when they violate it.

"Tell me more about *Curve Connection*," Megan says. "Do you like it so far?"

"I haven't really looked at it much. I started signing up today but chickened out," Maya says with a soft laugh.

I discreetly adjust my dick, fully aware that I'm an asshole for doing it. I can't help it though. That sweet laugh is like Kryptonite. It grabbed me by the cock as soon as I heard it and hasn't let go since. Which is odd in and of itself. He hasn't taken an interest in much for a good, long while.

He's certainly interested in Maya.

"Why?" Megan asks.

"I don't know. I'm just..." Maya huffs. "I guess I'm nervous. You guys know I've never dated. Between my mom, work, and school, I've never had time. I'm not even sure I have time *now*. But I just feel...."

"You're lonely," Megan says when she doesn't finish her sentence.

"Yeah," Maya sighs. "I see the way Nadia parents are with one another, and I want that for myself. I'm tired of going home to an empty house every night. But maybe a dating app is a bad idea. I don't have the energy to wade through married men or men who want to hookup."

"It's not a bad idea," Megan disagrees.

"Nope," Cassidy says.

"You're gorgeous, you're smart as hell, and anyone would be lucky to date you," Megan says, her voice soft. "Yes, there are jerks out there. But there are good guys too. I know you've been through a lot since your mom died, but you're never going to meet a good one if you don't put yourself out there. Just like with that guy on campus, the one you convinced yourself not to approach before the spring session ended. You had stars in your eyes over him, but you talked yourself out of taking a chance."

Poor baby. The fact that she's grieving her mom makes me want to scoop her up into my arms even more than I already did. I understand exactly how it feels to lose a parent. Losing my dad fucking sucked, still does.

And what fucking asshole on campus caught her eye? Whoever he is, he doesn't deserve her, and I already hate him.

"You're right," Maya says.

"We are?"

"Yes. I'm going to sign up."

"Yeah?" Cassidy asks.

"Yes!" Maya cries, laughing quietly.

"Tonight."

"Tomorrow. I need a long soak in a hot tub tonight."

Yeah, that'll be a big hell no from me. There's no way I'm letting her match with some random asshole on this dating app. He won't appreciate her nearly as much as she deserves. Like they said, men on the internet suck. So I'm heading that shit off at the pass and asking her out to dinner. For the next month straight. That'll keep her off the app long enough for me to claim her, right?

"Two months," I mumble to myself...just in case it takes her a while to fall for me. My sister loves to tell me that I'm an autocratic, grumpy bastard with no patience and even fewer social skills. She says it like it's a bad thing, but I fail to see the problem. I'm deferring to her wisdom this time, though. Just in case she has a point.

I tried dating a few times when I was younger. It never worked out. As it turns out, I enjoyed my job more than the few women I went out with. They didn't seem to care for that much. One informed me that I was an asshole when I told her that. She probably wasn't wrong. But fuck. It's not like I set out to offend her. Law, I understand. Women? Not so much.

My phone rings as I'm sliding out of the booth to go scoop Maya up before some asshole on this dating app sees her and tries to take her from me. That'll just piss me off. I don't play well with others, and I don't share.

"Dammit," I growl, fishing my phone from my pocket to see my Ma's number lighting up the screen. For a second, I think about ignoring the call. A second is all that thought last. My dad would kick my ass if he were still alive.

"Ma," I say, swiping to answer.

"Kane!"

Even though I'm short on patience, I smile when she says my name like she hasn't talked to me in five years. She's called me three times already today to ask for guidance on buying a sink. As if I know the difference between a farmhouse sink and an undermount. A sink is a sink if you ask me. But Ma is a rare breed. She's in her early sixties and ornery as hell. She's convinced I know everything...which is exactly how I got roped into helping her renovate.

"What kind of trouble are you causing now, Ma?" I ask.

"No trouble," she says. "But I just got off the phone with your sister. She has a show on Friday."

"I know. I promised her that I'd go." A crowded bar full of drunks isn't my idea of a good time, but I try to show up whenever I can to support Kenna. We may be fifteen years apart, but we've always been close.

"Oh, good! That new music manager of hers gives me the creeps," Ma says. "I don't like her being alone with him."

"Ma," I say, shaking my head. "She'll be in a bar full of people."

"And so was that poor college student who disappeared last week in Knoxville," she sniffs.

I wasn't aware there was a college student missing in Knoxville, but if anyone would know, Ma would. She's hooked on true crime. I've told her a thousand times that she needs to stop watching that shit because it makes her paranoid, but she never listens. Last month, she was certain her neighbor's son murdered her and was trying to cover it up. The month before that, she was convinced her best friend's husband was working for the mob.

Like I said, she's a rare breed.

"You're right," I say instead of arguing with her. It won't get me anywhere. Besides, she's met Kenna's new manager. I haven't. That's reason enough to make sure he's not fucking with my baby sister. "I'll check out the manager."

"You're such a good boy, dear."

I passed *boy* a long damn time ago. But there's no telling her that, so I don't even try.

"I'll call you tomorrow, Ma. I've got something to take care of."

"Stop by tomorrow. I made cookies."

"Peanut butter with chocolate chips?"

"Your favorite."

"I'll be there. Love you."

"Love you."

I hang up, already headed around the wall to the booth on the opposite side. Except Maya isn't there anymore. Neither are her friends. I quickly glance around the crowded restaurant, but don't see her anywhere.

"Fuck," I growl, drawing the attention of an elderly couple.

The old woman purses her lips at me.

I ignore her and spin on my heel, already reaching for my wallet. I quickly toss several bills on my table and then stride toward the doors, muttering apologies as I weave through the maze of occupied chairs standing between me and Maya. I don't know why restaurants put tables so close together. I'm six-five and bulky. I feel like a bull in a china shop trying to dodge diners.

Despite moving as quickly as possible, by the time I make it outside, I'm too late. There are cars parked all up and down the dark street, but I don't see Maya or her friends anywhere.

Fuck.

I should have ignored Ma's call and talked to Maya while I had the chance. Nashville's a big city. Without doing something unethical and looking up her personal information, the chances of me finding her again before classes resume are slim to none.

Except...I know one place she'll be for sure.

The dating app.

What the fuck did she say it was called? Curvy Connect? Connecting Curves?

"Curve Connection," I mutter. It was called *Curve Connection*. I've never used a dating app in my life, but it looks like I'm about to start. I have a curvy little lamb to find. Preferably before I have to kill some poor bastard for making the mistake of trying to touch what's mine. And make no mistakes about it, sweet little Maya is going to be mine.

# Chapter Two
## MAYA

"Daddy!"

"Don't run!" I call after Nadia Mikhail as she takes off toward her father in the pick-up line. Mateo Kirby follows behind her. I swear, the two of them are inseparable. Mateo follows her around like he's her shadow. It's adorable how close they are.

"Sorry, Miss Denver," Nadia calls back to me, immediately slowing to a walk.

Her dad, Knox, watches her carefully. He's so funny. He can't seem to decide if he likes Mateo or if he's suspicious of the boy for following Nadia everywhere. But he adores his daughters and makes no secret of it. He's a good father, one of the best. A lot of fathers aren't nearly as involved as he is, but he makes a point to show up for his girls.

Plus, his wife is amazing. I love Lauren to pieces. Nadia, too. Classes haven't been in session long, but she's already surpassed any and all expectations. She aces everything I put in front of her. She's not quite old enough for the gifted and talented program yet, so I've been working with her one-on-one to modify the curriculum so it's more challenging for her.

I wave once Knox scoops her up in a hug and then pats Mateo on the head, rumbling a thank you to the sweet boy. Knox lifts his chin in a nod to me, but Nadia and Mateo both wave goodbye. I wait until they're in the car with Nadia's little sister, and then double check to make sure the rest of my class is on the way home.

There are a few cars still in the pick-up line, waiting for their turn, but all twenty of my kids are where they're supposed to be for once. It doesn't happen often, but I'm glad it did today. I love my job and every single one of my students, but I've been anxiously awaiting the end of the day for hours. I was sure I was going to explode if it didn't end soon.

My next semester of grad school begins Monday, and I still have a million things to do this weekend. Trying to teach by day and go to school at night is a lot of work. But that's not even on my mind as I hurry back inside and then cut down the hall to my classroom. My heels tap against the hard linoleum floor, echoing down the hallway.

I keep my head down, trying to avoid getting caught in conversation. I may actually burst if I don't get to my phone soon. Three days ago, I let my best friends convince me to sign up for a dating app. *Curve Connection* specializes in making connections for plus-size women like myself. I must have been crazy to sign up. Like I told my besties, I don't even have enough time to sleep right now!

But that's not really why I hesitated to join the app. The truth is, I don't want to meet anyone else when there's only one man who makes my heart race and my belly quiver.

*Kane Maxwell.*

The first time I saw him on campus, I fell in love. He towered over everyone else, looking a little like a caged lion as he strode through the crowd. Everything about him is dark, from his hair to his obsidian eyes to the way he scowls like a thundercloud to his imposing stature. But he is so damn beautiful to me. He's broad through the shoulders with a barrel chest and legs the size of tree trunks. He isn't overweight, just solid. He looks more like he belongs on a football field than standing behind a podium or in a court room. There's a roughness in the set of his jaw, a wildness in those obsidian eyes.

Both fascinate me.

I couldn't look away from him that first day. I was rooted to the spot, awestruck. I'm a little embarrassed to admit how much time I've spent ogling him since then. He just gives me this feeling in my stomach, like I ate a pack of Poprocks and they're still bursting and fizzing in there. It's a dozen different sensations, all clamoring for attention at once.

It's a new feeling, one that's as thrilling as it is anxiety-inducing. The thought of being rejected by him makes my stomach hurt. It's also a very real possibility. He's a professor, and I'm a grad student. He's an actual adult, with his own law firm. I still eat Ramen in front of the television and sleep with a stuffed animal. Most days, I'm a complete mess.

I'm also a twenty-three-year-old virgin with no dating history. My mom was sick for a long time before she died, and I spent all of my time caring for her. I haven't even been kissed since the ninth grade! Before Kane, no one ever interested me enough to change that. When dating seems more like a chore than something to look forward to, it's probably not a good time to start. And it always seemed like a chore to me...just one more thing in a long list of things I was supposed to be doing as an adult woman.

Soaking up every minute with my mom was more important.

Dating Kane doesn't seem like a chore, though. It seems...heavenly. But my mom died last year, and I've been a bit of a mess since. I lost myself when I lost her and finding me again has been a journey. For a long time, I didn't think I'd ever stop crying myself to sleep every night. The thought of approaching him in the middle of grieving was mildly terrifying to me. So, I talked myself out of it doing it. If I never talked to him, he couldn't break my already grieving heart, right?

Wrong.

He's on the dating app.

*And he wants to match with me.*

I nearly swallowed my tongue in front of my entire class when I saw *Kane Maxwell wants to match with you!* light up my screen today. Somehow, for some reason, the Universe is giving me a second chance to talk to the man I've spent the last few months loving from afar.

There's only one problem. Come Monday, Kane Maxwell won't just be a random professor I see around campus. He'll be *my* professor. I swear, it wasn't intentional. I may be crazy about him, but I'm not crazy enough to sign up for his seminar just to stare at him.

How awkward would that be?

Super awkward.

And far bolder than I am.

But I missed an important educational law seminar last year when my mom died, and I need it to graduate. So I signed up for it this semester. Only I didn't know Kane was going to be my professor until a week ago. Any chance I had with him disappeared in a puff of smoke right then and there, which is why I joined the app in the first place. I thought maybe it would help me get over him. Or at least make me less likely to blurt out my feelings for him in front of the entire class.

But that was before he sent my world spinning into orbit today. Now, the little devil on my shoulder keeps trying to lead me right down the path to temptation. And I think I might be morally flawed because the longer it whispers in my ear, the more reasonable it sounds.

By the time I reach my classroom, most of the other teachers are already heading for the parking lot. I wave and then duck inside my room, not wasting the time on small talk. Ignoring the maze of chairs and little bits of paper littering the carpet, I go straight for my desk to pull out my phone. My hands actually shake with nerves when I open the *Curve Connection* app and scroll to my notifications.

*Kane Maxwell wants to match with you!*

I exhale a breath, a little relieved that I didn't just imagine it. I've never had a panic attack before, but I feel a little like I'm having one right now. My heart is racing a million miles a minute and my right eye keeps twitching.

*Get it together, Maya. You're a grown woman.*

Right.

I don't feel particularly grown right now.

I hover my finger over the notification, and then glance around like a big dork. I'm in my classroom alone. Of course no one is spying over my shoulder.

I tap the button to take me to his profile.

"Holy crap," I whisper when his photo comes up on the screen. It's definitely him. His dark head is bent toward his laptop. He's wearing reading glasses, with a hint of a smirk curving his full lips up on the right side. In the photo, he has a beard and mustache. They make his jaw look wickedly sharp. He seems relaxed, more than he ever does on campus.

I scroll through his profile, unable to resist. He's thirty-nine, born and raised in Nashville like me. He's only been on the app for a few days, but it doesn't look like he's matched with anyone yet. I'm a little relieved. I don't like the thought of him with someone else. It feels a little...corrosive. I'm guessing that's the jealousy eating away at me.

Had anyone told me six months ago that it was entirely possible to fall in love with a complete stranger, I probably would have laughed. And then I did exactly that with Kane. I am so in love with him it's a little bit pathetic.

His profile doesn't have a whole lot to it, but I devour every word. His bio reads, "Where are you, my sweet lamb?" I'm not sure why that makes me smile, but it does. It's a little bit of softness from a man who seems anything but soft to me. Underneath that gruff exterior, he's gentle, romantic.

I'm not really surprised. Kane is a lot of things that I find insanely attractive. I feel like I'm just figuring out who I am, but he's so confident and capable. He knows himself and doesn't really seem to care what anyone thinks about him. People respect him for it. Even though he's a bit of a grump, no one ever has anything bad to say about him.

"Likes hockey, classic literature, and 80s hairbands," I read aloud. "Dislikes crowds, renovations, and the asshole who invented paint." That part makes me laugh out loud. I'm guessing HGTV isn't high on his list either. That's fine with me. Manual labor and I aren't friends. I tried to fix the garbage disposal once and ended up on Noah's Ark.

Thank God for Bubba's Plumbing and a sympathetic landlord.

I click off Kane's profile and pull up my text app.

**Me: My guy from campus is on the app.
He wants to match me.**

I scroll back to his profile while waiting for Megan and Cassidy, my best friends, to text me back. Maybe they can talk the devil on my shoulder into behaving.

"Maybe not," I mutter, my eyes running over the picture of him again. He's so damn devilishly handsome. I want to know what it's like to be between those hands, under his command. I've thought about that more than once. How rough his palms would feel against my skin. How he'd sound, grunting my name while he's thrusting into me. How it would feel to have my hands in his dark hair while he's eating me. I've touched myself thinking about him so much I should be ashamed of myself.

I'm not ashamed. I have a Kindle and an unlimited supply of steamy romance at my fingertips. My mind is a shameless, dirty place when it comes to Kane Maxwell's fine self.

**Megan: The professor?**

**Me: Yes. Kane.**

I take a quick screenshot and drop it into our group chat.

**Cassidy: Damn. No wonder you're hung up on him.**

**Megan: Um, hello, daddy.**

**Me: What do I do?**

"Talk sense into me, please. I'm about to do something mad, bad, and a little bit wicked," I say aloud...but I leave that part out of my text. I don't want them to talk me out of matching with him, not really. Even if it's certain to end in disaster of Titanic proportions, I want this man.

**Megan: What do you want to do?**

What do I want to do? Match him. Date him. Have his babies.

Me: He's going to be my professor soon.

Cassidy: Exactly. As in, he isn't your professor now.

Megan: What she said. You're both adults. Besides, matching someone on an app isn't the same as dating them, hon. You guys may talk and realize you're not compatible.

Cassidy: You'll never know if you don't take the chance.

Megan: Does he know you're his student?

Me: I doubt it.

It usually takes a few weeks before they remember our names if they ever do. And I was just added to his seminar a week ago. I'm just a name in a long list of names to him. Besides, I'm on the app as Maya, but my legal first name is Mayani.

**Megan: This is your sign from the universe, hon.**

**Cassidy: Match him!**

I think my friends may be bad influences. They're not talking sense into me at all. I think they just perched on my shoulder with the devil.

**Megan: She means sleep with him.**

**Cassidy: That too.**

And I'm pretty sure they're sharing a bottle of vodka with him.

I swap back to the app, looking at Kane's photo again. Everything about him is ridiculously attractive to me.

Everything about him makes me ache in places that have never ached for anyone else. Surely that means something important. I don't know, but I never will if I don't take a chance.

I swipe to match with him, and then squeak and drop my phone. Which makes me feel like a dork all over again. It's not like he can see me swiping. Besides, just because we matched doesn't really mean anything.

Except...I desperately want it to mean something.

**Me: I did it.**

**Megan: YES!**

**Cassidy: Go, Maya!**

By *go*, I hope she doesn't mean straight to hell.

*Ding.*

"Shoot!" I cry, dropping a desk on my foot when my phone vibrates in my pocket. It hasn't even been ten minutes since I matched him. Less, actually. It feels like I've been waiting with bated breath for fifteen years. Megan and Cassidy tried to talk me into sliding into his DMs, but I ignored that suggestion. Matching him was hard enough! I wouldn't even know what to say.

*I've been obsessed with you for months* doesn't exactly roll off the tongue.

I quickly put the desk where it belongs and then hobble back to mine before pulling my phone out of my pocket. My heart leaps into my throat as soon as I see the notification from the app. My hands shake as I unlock my phone and pull the app up to read it.

**Kane: Sweet Maya, I need to know... If you're here, who's running heaven?**

I stare at his message for a long moment and then giggle. It's cheesy and ridiculous but also sweet at the same time. Far sweeter than I expected from someone who looks like he could give the devil a run for his money. I know he's a good guy. I guess I just expected him to always be grumpy like he is on campus.

**Me: I left Abel in charge.**

**Kane: Good choice. God always favored him.**

**Kane: Not to be forward, but you're fucking beautiful. That sweet smile bowled me over, baby girl.**

My stomach flutters, excitement firing through my system. He's flirting with me. He thinks I'm beautiful. Holy crap. If I'm dreaming, I never want to wake up again.

I hesitate for a second, not sure what to say back to him. And then inspiration strikes, and I go for it.

> **Me: You're not so bad yourself. If you were a Transformer, you'd be Optimus Fine.**

> **Kane: Nice. What else do you got?**

> **Me: If you were a fruit, you'd be a fine-apple.**

> **Kane: I think there's something wrong with my phone. Would you mind calling it?**

> **Me: Um, sure. What's your number?**

I wait for him to give it to me.

**Kane: It's a pick-up line, sweet Maya.**

**Me: Oh.**

My stomach twists. Even though he can't see me, my cheeks flame with embarrassment. Of course it's a pick-up line and he wasn't asking me to call him. I don't know how I'm in charge of people's actual children. I shouldn't even be in charge of myself!

**Kane: But you should absolutely call me so I can ask you out over the phone. I'd like to hear that sweet voice.**

"Oh my gosh," I whisper, my hands shaking when he immediately sends his number. I stare at it for a long time, my mind completely blank.

**Kane: Shit. Too soon?**

**Me: No. I'm just nervous. Um, I've never done this before.**

**Kane: So I'm your first, huh? I like the sound of that.**

**Me: I don't date much.**

**Kane: That's good news for me. I promise not to bite.**

My stomach flutters again. Though, I don't think it's nerves this time. The thought of him biting me is...sexy as hell, to be honest. There's something about being behind a screen that makes me feel bolder, braver.

**Me: What if I want you to bite?**

**Kane: You like playing with fire, huh?**

**Me: Maybe.**

**Kane: Truth is, I've been thinking about sinking my teeth into that gorgeous body for longer than I should admit. Would you slap me if I told you that my dick is rock hard for you right now, sweet Maya?**

Oh my gosh. I press the heel of my hand to my forehead, trying to cool myself down. It doesn't work. I feel like I'm on fire.

**Me: No.**

**Kane: Good because it's true. Full disclosure: I plan to fuck you. Repeatedly. But I'm not interested in a quick hookup. There's nothing quick about the things I'm going to do to you. And while I'm doing them, I plan to make you fall for me.**

Oh, wow. I set my phone on the desk and pinch my arm, just to make sure I'm awake and not dreaming any of this. I'm not because it hurts like hell when I catch my skin between my fingers and squeeze. This is really happening right now. Kane Maxwell wants to sleep with me. He wants me to fall for him.

What would he say if he knew I did that months ago?

**Kane: Call me, baby girl. Let me hear that beautiful voice.**

I dial his number before I can talk myself out of it. My heart beats so loud I hear it better than I do the single ring.

"Maya," Kane says as soon as he answers. His voice is a velvety growl of sound that's entirely wicked. It reminds me of a big cat purring. Right before it pounces. "You called."

"You asked me to," I remind him.

"I know. I just wasn't sure if you would or not."

"Oh."

"I know you just met me five minutes ago, but I want you to go out with me tonight," he says, not wasting any time. I like it. He gets right to the point. "I'll keep my hands to myself if that's what you want, but I want to see you."

I hesitate, torn between throwing caution to the wind and saying yes, and telling him the truth and saying no. Come Monday, this man will be my professor. I should tell

him that, right? Yes, of course I should. But I don't want
to tell him the truth.

Is it so wrong to want one night with this man before all
my fantasies die a quick death and I spend forever alone?
Maybe. But I want one night anyway.

"Say yes, baby girl," he murmurs. "I'm fucking dying to
see you."

"Yes," I blurt, securing my place in hell. It can't be much
worse down there than Nashville in the summer, right?
*Please don't be too mad, Baby Jesus. I promise I'll be good
from now on.*

"Thank fuck," he growls into the phone. "What's your
address?"

"Um...can I just meet you there?" I ask instead of giving
it to him. My apartment is tiny and sad. Paying my mom's
medical bills and paying for school isn't cheap. We're from
two different worlds. I'd rather him not see that up close
and personal before we even have a chance to talk.

"Good girl," he says, misunderstanding my hesitation.
"Never give your personal information to someone you
just met."

*We didn't just meet. I've been fantasizing about you for
months.*

"Okay," I whisper instead of telling him that.

"My sister has a show tonight at Rucker's. Do you know it?"

"The bar downtown?"

"Yes. Meet me there at eight."

"You want me to meet your sister?"

"Fuck no," he growls, sending my heart plummeting into my stomach. "God only knows what embarrassing shit she'll tell you. But I want to see you sooner rather than later. I've been fucking dying to see that smile since I first saw you."

"You mean my picture," I say, smiling over the fact that he's worried his sister will tell me embarrassing stories about him. There probably aren't very many.

"Right, your picture," he mutters.

When I still hesitate to agree, he grits out my name.

"Give me one chance, sweet Maya," he says. "We'll have a drink and get to know one another. You'll be safe with me. I won't push for anything you aren't ready to give me."

The devil on my shoulder whispers in my ear again. And I give into temptation.

"Yes," I say.

# Chapter Three
## KANE

"Kane!" Kenna says, throwing her arms around me in a big hug as soon as I step inside Rucker's. It's not even 7:30, and the place is already packed. And loud.

"Hey," I say, squeezing her back as my eyes run over the crowd. Despite the level of noise, they seem tame tonight. Thank God. Her last manager had her playing in some seedy places with rough crowds...which is precisely why he was fired. It was either that or try dislodging my size sixteen from his colon. I much prefer defending criminals to becoming one myself.

Jails aren't appealing.

"I'm so happy you came." Kenna beams up at me, her hazel eyes glowing with excitement. Her eye makeup is dark and smoky, her lips ruby red. Despite it, she looks younger than she is, fresh-faced in a way that's rare in this world. Kenna is...Kenna. She's an innocent little songbird who marches to the beat of her own drum. She's petite and curvy and has balls bigger than most men I know. She's also sweet and gentle and willing to do anything for the people she loves.

"I told you I'd be here, brat," I remind her, tapping her on the nose.

She chomps her teeth at me.

"Besides, Ma wanted me to check out your new manager."

"Don't you dare run him off, Kane David Maxwell," Kenna hisses at me, slamming her hands down on her hips. "He's an important man in the industry. I need him."

"We'll see," I say, making no promises. Kenna sees the best in everyone, regardless of whether they deserve it or not. Me? Not so much. I don't give a fuck if her new manager is God. If he's shady or fucks with my sister, he won't be her manager for long.

She growls at me, which makes me smile. She may be fearless, but I'm more than twice her size and a helluva lot less inclined to give a shit. As a musician, she needs people to like her. I don't have the same problem. I'm a lawyer. People never like us, which works out well for me since I don't like most people.

If I wasn't jaded before I went into law, it certainly tipped the scales. When presented with two choices, most people will, without fail, choose the one that panders to their own interests, regardless of who their decision might harm. To save their own asses, there isn't much most people won't do. I always thought I was different. But as it turns out, I'm willing to do a lot of shady shit myself when it comes to a certain raven-haired beauty. Like eavesdrop, join a dating app, jerk off to her photo six times in a row....

I may be a bastard, but at least I'm honest about my flaws. Most people aren't. They do all sorts of mental gymnastics to keep from facing hard truths. People assume that laws are what keep society functioning, but they're wrong. It's fear of consequences that keeps most people on the straight and narrow. Remove the fear, and they're willing to do any number of illegal and immoral things. I've seen the same story play out a thousand times, in a thousand different ways, to a thousand different ends.

Liking Bob when he's smiling in your face is one thing. It's a lot harder when you know he's fucking his wife's sister behind her back. Karen seems great when she's rallying the troops to support her kid's class. She's a helluva lot less likable when you know she's been stealing from the PTA for years and drinks herself into a stupor every night.

My job requires me to see behind the masks people wear on a daily basis. And, quite frankly, most of them are assholes underneath. But I don't get paid to like them. I don't even get paid to believe the shit they say. I get paid to defend their shit choices when said shit choices land them in front of a judge and a jury of their peers.

Kenna is different. She's an idealist. If being an asshole allows her to keep those rose-colored glasses, then I'll happily be an asshole. She doesn't have to like it. Most of the time, I'm sure she doesn't. But she loves me anyway. It's her familial obligation.

"Kenna."

I glance up to see a man about my age headed in our direction. He's maybe five-six, with slicked back hair and beady eyes. I know on sight that he's the new manager. He's in a suit, for one. And he's wearing the same slick smile every other manager she's had wears. It's like the damn thing comes standard issue. His beady eyes flick over me. I can practically see him weighing my value. He dismisses me as unimportant almost immediately.

Prick.

"The stage manager has a few questions for you," he says to my sister, still smiling at her.

Ma was right. He is creepy. And I doubt the stage manager wants to see her. He just doesn't like that she's talking to me. I see the jealousy in his eyes. Bad news for him, but he won't be touching my sister if he plans to keep those hands of his. I have no problem ripping them off and shoving them up his own ass.

Either my opinion shows on my face, or my sister knows me too well. Before I can say anything, she elbows me in the stomach. Hard.

I double over, cursing under my breath.

"Of course," she says to the manager. "Um, John, this is my brother, Kane. Kane, this is my manager, John."

"Oh, you're the brother," John says. This time, he doesn't dismiss me. He slaps an even brighter smile on his face and holds out his hand for me to shake. Fucker.

"Hey," I grunt, scowling at him. I don't shake his hand.

Kenna stomps on my foot.

"Goddamn," I growl at her. "Would you stop doing that?"

"Doing what?" She bats her lashes at me. Little shit.

"It's nice to meet you. We'll have to talk later," John says, still giving me that salesman smile. His teeth are too white. It makes him look fake. "Kenz, I'll see you backstage in two."

"Kenz?"

"I've gotta go talk to the stage manager," she says as soon as he wanders off, ignoring my question. "I'll see you when I take a break."

I grab her arm before she can rush off. "Do me a favor and behave tonight. I have a date."

I didn't think I stood a chance in hell of getting Maya to agree to go out with me, and I don't want anything to fuck it up. When she matched me today, I didn't waste any time messaging her. I've been going out of my mind, trying to find her on the app before someone else did. It took a lot longer than expected since I didn't have her last name. For a new app, it's popular.

I've been swiping for three days. Everyone except Maya got a no.

Kenna spins to face me, her mouth hanging open. "Seriously?"

"Yeah." I narrow my eyes on her. "You better behave."

"I'll behave if you will," she says, smirking at me.

I frown, which only makes her smirk grow.

"Fine," I growl. "I won't run off your manager tonight."

"Then I won't tell your date about the time you puked on Superman," she says, lifting up on her toes to plant a kiss on my cheek. "Bye!"

I watch her hurry off, shaking my head. God save whichever poor bastard marries her. He's going to have his hands full trying to keep her out of trouble. I should know. I've been doing it most of my life. It's the sole reason I'm in danger of going gray at thirty-nine. Well, that and renovating Ma's fucking house.

Once Kenna is out of sight, I wade through the crowd to a booth off to the side. It's in a dark corner, but I can see both the stage and the door from it, which works well for me. My ass no more hits the wooden bench before a waitress materializes in front of me.

"Hey, handsome. What can I getcha?" she asks, her gaze raking up and down my body.

"Two waters," I growl, ignoring her blatant perusal. There's only one woman I'm interested in, and this one isn't her. "And two of whatever beer you have on tap."

She jerks her chin in a nod and then scurries off.

As soon as she moves, I see Maya walking in the door.

"Fuck me," I groan, a fist of desire hitting me in the solar plexus. She's even more beautiful than I remember. She's wearing a tiny white dress with a jean jacket and cowboy boots. Her wild hair hangs loose around her round face. If she's wearing makeup, I can't tell.

At least two dozen different men turn to look at her when she pauses in the doorway. They scent her innocence like she's prey. It practically drips from her as she nervously smooths her dress down over her wide hips. I don't have to see their faces to know what they're thinking as they watch her. Too fucking bad for them. This one is mine, and I won't ever share her.

I climb to my feet, wading across the bar toward her.

I'm halfway there when she notices me.

Her eyes crawl up my body, turning glassy. She gulps almost audibly.

Damn, she's beautiful. And she's looking at me like I'm something special. To most women, I'm either a bucket list item or someone to be avoided. They're split down the middle on whether my size is attractive or makes me dangerous. It's a pain in the ass, but I get it. Women are raised to be cautious around men they don't know, especially ones who tower over them like I do. Maya isn't looking at me like she's afraid of me though. Nor is she looking at me like I'm a tree she wants to climb. She's looking at me like she can't look away.

That makes two of us.

As I cross the crowded bar to her, I don't see anything but that sweet face. My heart thumps unevenly against my ribcage, pounding out a rhythm that I feel deep in my bones.

*Mine. Mine. Mine mine mine.*

God, yeah, she is. She has no clue just how *mine* she is.

"Maya," I murmur, reaching for her hand as soon as I'm standing in front of her. Her scent swirls around me—the tiniest hint of vanilla. I pull it into my lungs, inhaling it like the greedy bastard I am.

She holds one delicate hand out to me like she's in a dream, moving on instinct. I feel a little like I'm in a dream too. One where the rest of the world exists entirely outside of this moment. We're in our own world, speaking our own language. I want to stay right here in it for the rest of my life. Fuck the outside world. All I need is this woman and that sweet smile.

Her fingers slip through mine, sending a shower of sparks up and down my spine. They pop like fireworks, bursting in a spray of fire as it rains down on me. My cock turns to steel, pressing insistently against the fly of my pants. When we're palm to palm, I realize what I didn't until just now. That primal, wild part of me isn't just saying *mine*. He's saying *hers* too.

Fuck, I can't wait to belong to this sweet little thing. She'll lead me around by the cock and I'll love every second of it. I almost feel sorry for her for getting saddled with a grumpy motherfucker like me. But I plan to make it worth the hassle for her.

"You look beautiful," I murmur, tugging her until she's so close we're damn near hugging it out right where we stand. It's forward and probably rude as fuck, but I bend down, skimming my nose along the side of her face. I inhale her sweet scent again, reveling as it spreads through my system in warm waves. "I was worried you wouldn't come."

She shivers in my arms, and I know she feels it too. The spark. The connection. Desire. Whatever it is that makes me want to fuck her up against the door in one breath and then cuddle her close in the next. I didn't understand that second desire until I heard that she lost her mom recently, and then I got it. This sweet little lamb is lost, grieving, and alone in the world. Every instinct I have demands I watch over her while she finds her way.

It's not a charitable instinct. Not entirely. I want to be the man who helps her find her way because the thought of letting anyone else do it pisses me off. Something in me recognizes something in her. She's necessary. Important. Whichever word means *mine* in polite society.

"Kane," she whispers. Her voice shakes with nerves. Hopefully with desire too. I know I'm not the only one feeling it. Her little nipples are hard, gooseflesh covering her arms. She's entirely too beautiful to be real, and yet she is.

I want to taste those pouty lips more than I want my next breath, but I manage to pull myself back, trying not to move too fast for her. She said she's never done this before, and I know she means more than using a dating app. I eavesdropped on her conversation the other night, shamelessly memorizing every word. If she's not a virgin, she's close to it. Innocent in every sense of the word. I don't want to spook her into running.

"I got us a table," I say, sliding my arm around her waist to move us deeper into the room. My gaze drifts around, satisfaction coursing through me when I see that everyone else has taken their eyes off of her. They know she's mine now, and they're either smart enough to realize that means she's off-limits, or they're too drunk to see her clearly.

"Thank you," she says.

I lead her across the bar and then help her slide into the booth. She squeaks, practically falling into it while trying to keep her dress down over her hips. Heat climbs up her cheeks. I smile at the sight. She really is a sweet little lamb.

I've never wanted to be the big, bad wolf more than I do right now.

*Kane, what a big cock you have. Yes, lamb. All the better to fuck you with.*

"Sorry," she says, her eyes on the table. "I'm a little clumsy."

I crook a finger beneath her chin, forcing her to look at me. "You're perfect," I correct, my eyes locked on hers. They're so damn green. Jesus. It's a little like looking into an emerald and seeing forever staring back. "Never apologize to me for being you, Maya. You're perfect."

"I..." She sinks her teeth into her bottom lip and then nods. "Okay."

I release her and then slide into the booth beside her.

"So I can hear you over the music," I say by way of explanation.

She smiles at me, and I know she knows I'm full of shit. She doesn't call me out on it though. If anything, she looks...satisfied. Like she's pleased I want to be as close to her as humanly possible.

"I ordered you a beer," I say, nudging the bottle toward her. Regardless of how I move, the damn table digs into my knees. But fuck it. I've got a pretty little baby doll tucked up beside me, a beer in front of me, and my sister about to take the stage. I'm golden.

"Thanks," Maya says, smiling at me. She wraps her hand around the bottle and takes a small sip.

I curse and readjust positions, trying to give my dick a little breathing room. It doesn't help.

"Tell me all about you, Maya," I say.

"What do you want to know?"

"Everything."

She gives me a sweet smile. "There isn't much to tell," she says with a self-conscious laugh. "Um, I teach fourth grade at JP Hall Elementary. I like reading. Hockey is my favorite sport."

"What team?"

"The Predators. Obviously," she says.

"Good girl."

She beams at me again. And Christ, I want to see that smile first thing every morning for at least the next ninety years. It's so full of warmth. When she smiles, the sadness in her eyes dims, as if in those moments, it holds no sway over her heart.

"You too, huh?"

"I was born and raised here. I think it's against the law not to support the home team."

"You would know, wouldn't you, Mr. Big Shot Lawyer?" she teases.

"More like Mr. Financially Solvent Lawyer," I say with a snort and then take a pull from my beer bottle. "Renovating my Ma's house takes too much time for me to be a big shot."

"Is that why you hate the guy who invented paint?" she asks. That crystalline laugh burbles from her lips. I've never wanted to be a sound more than I do right now.

"Not on friendly terms with the asshole who invented plumbing either," I grunt, making her laugh again. "I don't even know how the fuck I got roped into doing the grunt work. I know fuck-all about renovations."

"I think it's sweet," she says.

"Yeah?"

She bobs her head in a nod, her eyes sliding away from mine as heat climbs up her cheeks again. I want to trace that blush with my tongue, but I settle for tracing it with a single fingertip. She is so damn pretty. I feel like I won the lottery here.

"Have you ever heard of the Blombos Cave?" she asks.

"Doesn't sound familiar."

"It's a cave in South Africa," she says. "It's over one-hundred-thousand years old. That's where paint was first used. They even found the tools that were used to grind the ochre up into paint. So unless you have a really good time machine..."

"Guess I better get to work on that," I mutter, and then cock my head to the side, impressed. She's smart. I'm not really surprised. Intelligence blazes in those gorgeous eyes of hers. "You a history buff, baby girl?"

"Not really. My mom was always convinced that I had a photographic memory," she says. "If I did, I probably wouldn't lose my phone so much. But I just remember things I read...and I like to read. A *lot*."

"Your mom died." It's not really a question, but she takes it as one.

"Yeah," she says, her voice soft. "She passed away a little over a year ago. Ovarian cancer."

"Damn," I whisper. "I'm sorry, baby girl."

"Me too. I miss her like crazy." She takes a sip from her bottle, trying to hide the way her bottom lip quivers, but I see it. It breaks my heart for her. Kenna was about the same age when we lost my dad. It was as hard for her as it was for Ma. I can't imagine her having to grieve alone. It kills me to know Maya's been facing that yawning chasm of grief by herself for the last year.

"We lost my dad two years ago," I murmur, pulling her closer to me on the bench. I want to pick her up and put her in my lap, but figure that'll probably embarrass her or freak her out. She melts into me though, letting me slide an arm around her waist. "He had a massive heart attack."

"I'm so sorry," she whispers, tilting her head back to look at me. "Losing a parent is a special kind of awful, isn't it?"

"Yeah, it is. It's been especially tough on my Ma. They were high school sweethearts. Married as soon as they graduated. She thought they'd grow old together. Instead, she's trying to navigate it all by herself."

"Oh, wow," Maya whispers. "That has to be so hard for her."

"It is. But she keeps busy renovating her house. It's a pain in the ass, but it makes her happy," I say with a shrug. I may bitch about it, but I'll renovate fifteen of the damn things if it makes losing my dad easier for her. "The first few weeks, she didn't even get out of the bed."

Sympathy washes through Maya's expression. "Your poor mom. My mom never married. Um, I was the product of a one-night stand when my mom was my age. She was a little wild until she had me. And then she said she was too busy being a mom to worry about falling in love, so it was always just the two of us."

"No siblings?" I check, just to confirm what I've already worked out for myself.

She shakes her head.

"Damn, baby girl." I link our fingers and bring her head up to my mouth to kiss her knuckles. "I'm sorry. Losing her must have been hard on you."

"So hard," she whispers, and then she sucks in a deep breath and shakes her head as if she's shaking it off. She gives me a bright smile. This one doesn't dim the sadness in her eyes though. That lingers. "But I'm okay now."

"You're not," I disagree.

She deflates like a balloon. "That obvious, huh?"

"Nah," I reassure her. "I just know grief when I see it. I've been looking at it in the mirror for the last two years. My dad was always my hero. He was Mr. Big Shot Lawyer. He owned the family firm and made running it look like a breeze. It's a helluva lot harder than it looks. I wish like hell that he was here to tell me how he did it all."

"You own his firm now?"

I nod.

"And you teach."

"Part-time," I say.

"Well, I think you're doing a pretty good job living up to his example," she says.

"Yeah?" I pause when the waitress from earlier approaches to ask if we need anything else. "You hungry, baby girl?"

"Not really. I actually ate before I came," she says, giving me an apologetic grimace. "I wasn't sure if we were going to eat or not."

"Shit. I should have taken you for food first."

"It's okay," she promises, smiling at me. "At least this way, you don't end up with a date who is wearing half her food. White doesn't hide stains very well."

"Wouldn't bother me," I growl. "You'd still have my dick hard enough to pound steel."

The waitress's eyes go wide. So do Maya's.

"Shit," I say. "I forgot we weren't alone."

"It's okay," Maya says, but I can tell by the heat in her cheeks that she's embarrassed.

"We're good for now," I mutter to the waitress, feeling like an ass. Maybe Kenna is right about me having no social skills. "I shouldn't have said that."

"It's okay," Maya whispers, not looking me in the eye.

"I embarrassed you."

"What?" Her gaze flies to mine. "No, it's not that," she rushes to assure me. "I mean, I didn't expect you to say that, but I'm...flattered. I just...um..." She fidgets, clearly struggling to say whatever she wants to say. "I guess I just wonder.... Did you mean it?"

"Did I...?" I stare at her for a long moment, caught off-guard by the question. I haven't been able to keep my eyes off her since she walked in the door. I figured it was blatantly obvious by now that this gorgeous woman has me all twisted up in knots and aching for her. I've thought about little else since I saw her the other day. But maybe my feelings aren't as transparent as I thought.

"Let me see your hand," I demand, already reaching for it. I wrap my fingers around her wrist and pull her hand down to my lap. "Feel that, Maya?" I growl, pressing her hand to my dick, not giving a shit who sees. Letting her doubt how much I want her is intolerable to me. "He's been like that since you walked in the door. If we were alone right now, your pretty dress would be all fucked up and you'd be screaming my name."

"I..." She trails off, sitting completely still for a moment. But she doesn't pull her hand away. She doesn't slap me across the face either. She just stares at me for a long, breathless moment.

And then she wraps that perfect little hand around me and squeezes.

"Fuck," I growl, arching toward her touch.

"Kane?" she whispers. "What if I want to be alone with you right now?"

"Yeah? You want me, baby girl?"

"Yes," she says, meeting my gaze.

I should tell her no. Rationally, I know this. We need to talk about the fact that I'm a professor and she's a student. I need to come clean about eavesdropping on her conversation the other day. There are about fifteen different things we need to discuss before I get inside her, because there won't be another after me. But I don't say any of those things.

She's stroking me through my pants in the middle of a bar, and the only thing I can think about is the fact that I need in her more than I need my next breath. We can work out the particulars later. They won't change anything. This curvy little lamb is mine. God help anyone who thinks otherwise.

# CHAPTER FOUR
## MAYA

"You want me to fuck you, Maya?" Kane growls in my ear. "You ready to be mine?"

*Yes and yes, a thousand times yes.* I don't care if we're moving at the speed of light. It doesn't seem fast enough to me. I've thought of nothing else for months now. Knowing he feels the same way, that he wants me as badly as I want him...I don't want to wait or go slow or sit in this bar all night while he tries to be a gentleman and keep his hands to himself.

I want him naked and on top of me. Sooner rather than later.

"Yes," I whisper, still working him through his slacks. He is so damn big. I already know he's going to split me in half. The thing is though, I *want* him to do it. More than I think I've ever wanted anything. Even if it's only for tonight, I want to know what it feels like to belong to this incredible man.

He growls my name and lurches to his feet, his movements full of impatience. His dark eyes are on fire, burning with wicked intent and deadly desire. He thrusts a hand into his pocket and pulls out his wallet, not even looking as he tosses several bills on the table. He reaches for his phone with the other, his fingers flying across the screen as he taps out a text. To his sister? I don't know. I don't care who he's texting. Because within seconds, his phone is back in his pocket and he's reaching for my hand.

I allow him to draw me to my feet, trembling, shaking. God, I feel like I'm going to explode into a million tiny pieces if I don't feel him all over me right now. It's a little scary how much I want him. It's as if all those months of secret desire have coalesced, piling up like train cars after a wreck. There are sixty other people in the bar, but he's the only thing I see. He has been since I walked in the door.

My whole life, I've been a good girl and did what was expected. I threw myself into my education and lost myself in caring for my mom as she went through one round of chemo after another. I've been the obedient daughter, the model student, the ideal teacher. But I've never been *free*. I've never reached for what I wanted or stepped a toe out of line. Tonight, I don't want to be good. I don't want to do what's expected. I want to do...well, Kane Maxwell.

The air around us is charged, heated to the nth degree. I know he wants me the same way. Not just because he's rock hard, but because of the way he keeps looking at me. It's like he can't keep his eyes off me either. We're like magnets, drawing one another closer and then closer still.

"Careful, lamb," he croons, gripping onto me when I stumble into him.

I bite my lip to stifle a cry. His body feels incredible against mine. He's a veritable giant next to me, sexy in ways I can't even begin to describe. There's the heat of his body against mine. And the rough rasp of air as he pulls it into his lungs and then expels it against my skin. The roughness of his fingertips as they glide up and down my arms. Every little thing about him acts like an aphrodisiac on my system, overloading and short-circuiting it until all that's left is base desire.

Want.

Need.

Take.

That's all I can think about, like *Buffy* in that one episode.

Monday isn't a problem in this moment. It's been set aside, forgotten. I'll deal with it again later, when I don't feel like I'm going to explode apart beneath the maelstrom swirling through my veins. Right now, the only thing I can think about is him. And about how damn wet I am for him.

"Come on," he growls when I whimper his name, silently begging him to get me out of here before I do something I can't take back. Before everyone in this room sees just how desperate I am for this man.

I stumble along at his side, secure in his grip. Somehow, he hides me from the rest of the room, keeping me tucked up against him like he's never going to let me go. No one has a chance to see how my hands shake and my face flushes. He won't let them see me. He's my dark knight, standing head and shoulders above the crowd, a warning growl rumbling in his chest.

I gasp when he wrenches the door open. Cool air caresses my overheated skin. I bite my tongue to keep from crying out at this new sensation. It's too much and not enough at the same time. I see little more than flashes and blurs as he pulls me around the side of the building toward the parking garage. Neither of us says anything.

Loud laughter spills from the bar, but it sounds muted and far away. The headlights of cars passing on the street seem far away too. So do the sounds of people walking up and down the sidewalk all around us. Downtown Nashville at night is booming. Tourists, locals, and everyone in between descends on the area to enjoy all it has to offer.

As soon as we make it to the parking garage, my knight vanishes. Between one step and the next, Kane shifts from protector to hungry male. My chest collides with the cool cement wall as he spins me around, positioning his body behind mine. He presses up against me, just enough so I feel every inch of him. His erection nestles between my cheeks, his chest to my back.

"You keep making that sound, I'll be fucking you right here, Maya," he growls in my ear.

I open my mouth to ask what sound and then I hear myself. I'm whimpering. Moaning. I'm not sure which it is, but it's a barely audible purr of sound. I didn't even realize I was making it.

"Kane," I whisper, writhing between him and the wall. "Please. I need you."

"Fuck," he curses.

His hand around my throat sets me ablaze. I burn willingly, begging for more.

He turns my head just enough to be able to reach my mouth. His comes down on mine, silencing my pleas. He holds me firmly in his grip as he takes my mouth in a punishing kiss. It's heaven and hell at the same time. Heaven because I've wanted his mouth on mine for so long. Hell because I could have had this months ago if only I'd been a little bit braver.

I wasted so much time, convincing myself that I was too much of a mess for a man like him. Instead, I think I'm exactly the right kind of mess for a man like him. At least, he kisses me that way, like I'm something he can't live without. He growls when he can't get deep enough and spins me around. My back hits the wall and then he's all over me again.

And good god! This man knows how to kiss. I don't have much experience, but it's not necessary to judge the quality of this kiss. It's hot enough to liquefy my veins, turning the blood running through them into pockets of steams. The steam hisses as it roars through me.

I cling to him, my nails locked down on his muscular shoulders, trying to keep from falling into a puddle at his feet. He tastes like mint and beer. Underneath is another note, one that's uniquely him. It's hot and spicy and instantly addictive.

One rough hand skirts down my side, landing on my bare thigh. He growls into my mouth, slipping it beneath the hem of my dress.

"Gotta feel you," he mutters, already working his way up my inner thigh. My breath stalls in my throat as anticipation builds to a breaking point. His thumb brushes over the seam of my panties, just hard enough to jiggle my clit.

I cry out as an orgasm crashes over me out of nowhere. One minute, I feel like I'm going to die if he doesn't touch me soon. The next, I'm clinging to him, riding the waves as they break over me again and then again. It happens too fast to even think about holding it off.

"Jesus Christ," he growls. "You're coming, aren't you?"

"Y-y-yes," I manage to gasp.

He growls my name, tugging my panties to the side. We're steps away from the street, barely even out of sight, and I'm coming like we're alone in my room. He's touching me like we're alone in his. His thumb parts my slit, homing in on my clit.

"Do it again, baby girl. Come all over my fingers," he demands.

As if I could stop myself. Feeling his bare hand on me where no one has ever touched sets me off again. I fall into him, biting down on his shoulder to keep from crying out his name as fireworks detonate in my belly again and again. Pow. Pow. Pow.

By the time they finally stop, I'm gasping for breath, and I can't feel my fingertips or my toes. My heart pounds like a drum, banging against my ribcage so hard it's jarring. Part of me is in a fugue state, hovering miles off the ground. The rest of me is right here in the moment, jittery with excitement and the high of it all. Anyone could have seen us. That probably shouldn't turn me on as much as it does.

Kane holds me close, crooning praises in my ear. Somehow, they don't sound unnatural in that deep growl of his. They sound exactly right. He *feels* exactly right.

I'm in so much trouble with him. All this time, I tried to convince myself that I'd get over him. But I don't think I was being honest with myself. The way I feel about him is too big. Even if I waited fifty years, I'd still want him with the same piercing intensity.

Somehow, he's exactly the man I knew he would be. Only he's a thousand times better too. As impossible as it seems, I think I was meant to be his. I just didn't let myself believe that he could ever feel it too. How could I when it seemed so impossible? Love at first sight is supposed to be a fairytale. But either I'm living in Fantasia, or I was sorely mistaken on that front.

"You come that quick often, Maya?" Kane asks a moment later, pulling back to look at me.

I shake my head no, a little embarrassed at how quickly it happened.

His grin lets me know he doesn't mind. So does the heat in his eyes. "You're going to be doing that a lot more if you go home with me," he says, running his hands down my back. "I plan on keeping you coming until dawn, lamb. If you aren't ready for that, say no now. If you don't, I'm not sure I'll be able to keep my hands off you."

The fact that he's not pressuring me tumbles another little piece of my heart right into his hands. He's been hard all night, still is, but he isn't rushing me. If I say no, I have no doubt that he'll take me back inside. We'll drink beer, watch his sister perform, and talk the night away. But that's not what I want. Not right now. Not tonight.

"Kane?" I whisper, tilting my head back against the wall. I slide one hand through the hair at the nape of his neck, tugging gently. "Please don't keep your hands off me."

"Goddamn," he growls, his dark eyes heating again. "You sure, Maya? If all you want to do tonight is get to know one another, I'm happy with that, lamb."

"That's not what I want," I say, shaking my head. "I want you inside me. I want...I want you to be my first."

"Fuck," he swears, his nostrils flaring. His hand flexes around my hip. "You better be careful offering me that cherry, little girl. I'll fuck it right out of you and not feel sorry about it."

"That's kind of the plan, isn't it?" I ask, and then giggle when I see his face. He's so damn sexy, looking at me like I'm his next meal. He also looks miserable, like he only just realized that I'm one hundred percent on board with this plan of his and we're nowhere close to a bed.

I realize then what I never considered before. I'm not the only one a little awestruck here. I've been thinking he's out of my league, but I think he's been thinking the same thing about me. That realization makes me feel powerful, desirable. And a little bit naughty too.

"Take me home, Kane," I whisper, leaning up on my toes to press my chest against his. "I need you inside me before I go crazy."

He doesn't make me ask again.

He scoops me into his arms bridal style, making me squeal with delight. I throw my arms around his neck, hanging on for dear life as he storms across the dark parking garage like a bull. No, he's not my dark knight right now. He's all devil.

And he's all mine.

Neither of us says much on the way to his house, but I feel compelled to speak when we pull up out front. He lives on the edge of one of the more historic neighborhoods in Nashville. His house is a two-story Greek revival with large columns on each side of the porch. The second-story balcony rests between them. It's a lovely home with a big yard and rosebushes everywhere. Ivy climbs up trellises all along the side of it.

It's charming and elegant at the same time, as beautiful as the other homes in the community. It's a family home, the kind of place you raise a bunch of kids. Not at all what I would have expected for someone like him.

"Your house is beautiful, Kane," I say. I think my entire apartment would fit on the front porch, and still leave a little room to spare.

"It's not actually mine," he says, pulling to a stop just outside. "My parents lived here before my dad passed. But

Ma couldn't stand the thought of staying here with so many memories of him, so she put it on the market."

"You grew up here?"

He nods beside me. "I bought the place from her when she decided to move. Figured she might change her mind someday and regret giving it up."

"Kane," I whisper, my heart melting. There aren't many men who would buy their childhood home just to keep it for their grieving mom. The fact that he adores his so much makes me happy. My mom was always my best friend. I love knowing that he's so close to his.

"Seemed like the right thing to do," he says with a shrug, as if it's not the sweetest thing I've ever heard.

"You're a big teddy bear, aren't you?" I ask, smiling at him. I always thought I was a little crazy for being so certain that he was a genuinely good man, but nothing I heard ever changed my mind or swayed that opinion. He may be gruff and grumpy and say exactly what he's thinking, but he's also a brilliant lawyer and a phenomenal professor. Everyone respects him, even if they do find him a little bit intimidating. That says a lot about the kind of man he is. So does the fact that he dotes on his mom and shows up to support his sister.

I feel safe with him in a way I never have before. With him, I feel like it's okay to just be me, grief, messes, and all. He's a literal giant among men, one everyone has heard about even if they've never met him...yet he's not cocky or arrogant or self-centered. A lot of men in his position are full of themselves. Not Kane. He's simply...Kane.

Okay, maybe he's a *little* cocky, but that's not necessarily a bad thing. I think it's sexy that he knows exactly who he is and exactly what he likes. He says what he means and means what he says and doesn't much care if anyone else agrees or not. That confidence is attractive as hell to me.

"Come on," he says, hitting the button on the dash to switch off the ignition. And then he pops his door open and climbs out.

I take a deep breath, trying to calm my nerves. It doesn't work. His car smells like him, all spicy and sexy and delicious. That scent works like a wrecking ball on my composure, leaving me jittery and aching...just like I have been all night. This man is exactly the right everything to me.

He pulls my door open and then holds out a hand to help me to my feet. As soon as I place my hand in his, the same electrical current that's been there all night flares to life between us again. I know he feels it too because he grits out a curse, pulling me close to his body.

He's still hard. I feel his erection against my stomach.

"Maya," he growls when I slip my hand between us, running my knuckles over his erection.

"Kane," I say back, daring him to stop me.

He doesn't. He stands stock still as I touch him, marveling at how damn hard he is. At how big he is. At how badly I want him inside me, stealing my breath with every thrust. I already know he will. He's too damn big to be entirely gentle. That's all right though. I want him however he comes, for as long as he'll have me.

It's far too late to guard my heart against him. If he ends this come Monday, it'll rip my heart into tiny pieces. One night isn't enough. One weekend isn't either. I want forever. But if I can't have that...I plan to glut myself on him tonight. Just in case.

The sound of his zipper inching down seems loud to me. So does the way blood oozes through my veins, thick with desire. The wind rustles through the treetops. It's the only other sound on the dark street as I slip my hand inside his pants right there in his driveway, touching him the way he touched me.

Only, he doesn't come all over my hand. He doesn't even move as I wrap my fingers around his shaft, fumbling along. He's rock hard and silky smooth at the same time. Every thick inch of him is burning hot. The slit on the fat head is coated with sticky moisture. More spills across my knuckles when I twist my wrist to touch the underside of his cock. He's so thick, I can already feel him taking my breath. My hand doesn't close around him. It can't.

"You're going to break me in half with this, aren't you?" I ask, feeling brave and daring and a little bit wicked in the dark. With him watching over me, I discover a part of myself I've never had a chance to meet before. The wild woman who takes what she wants and makes no apologies. The wanton seductress who knows exactly how to drive her lover crazy.

"Depends," he growls, the first sound he's made since he said my name.

"On what?"

"On whether I have to let you leave my bed come morning," he says. "Because if I don't, you won't be able to walk, sweet lamb."

"And if you do?" I ask, still stroking him, trying to work out the perfect rhythm. His body guides me. The sharp intake of his breath, the way he cants his hips forward, the soft groan when I squeeze a little harder. I let his response guide me, opening every sense to him. I want to learn him in a way no one else ever has before. I don't want to know what he likes. I want to know what makes him crazy.

"If I do, you're going to feel me between your legs with every step you take," he growls.

"Kane," I moan.

"Don't worry, baby girl," he says, his voice like sandpaper in the dark. "Once I've played with you for a little while, I'll put you in the tub. It'll help ease the ache I plan to leave behind."

I'm no longer sure who is seducing who here. He's not even touching me, yet his words are wrecking me one by one. If I had any inhibitions left after the parking garage, they're floating away on the wind. This man is dangerous, exactly like a caged lion. Only this is one lock I want to break. One wild animal I want to set free.

"You should know," he says, speaking quietly, "I don't intend on letting you go. So if this is just one night to you, you're going to be sorely mistaken when I fuck my kid into you tonight, Maya. I decided to keep you before I ever touched you."

He's not joking. I hear it in his voice. An iron thread that says he means every word, that he won't be talked down or overruled on this. He's calling the shots here. And he wants me.

"W-why?" I ask.

"Which reason do you want, baby girl? The one that makes me sound like a gentleman or the truth?"

"The truth."

"Because you're the sweetest little lamb I've ever set eyes on," he says. "Because my dick hasn't been this hard in years. Because you've got me all tangled up in knots. *Because I can.*" He moves then, coming at me like a storm. His arms lash around me, hauling me up against his chest. His dick slips from my hand. Before I can cry out in loss, his mouth is on mine again.

He kisses me hard and deep, thrusting his tongue into my mouth in a preview of what's to come. If it's anything like this, I'm in serious trouble. My whole life, I've always thought I had self-control and willpower. I studied my ass off, even when doing it meant giving up the things I'd rather be doing. He flips that belief on its head and leaves me reeling.

When it comes to him, I have no control. I'm desperate and greedy, ruled entirely by base desire and those parts of myself I was always a little too afraid to face. That part of me isn't a mess. She's fiercely sexual and wildly untamed. She knows exactly who and what she wants. Kane Maxwell. And she's willing to play dirty to get him.

"Kane," I moan, practically climbing up his body to get closer to that wicked mouth.

He grunts and boosts me up, allowing me to wrap my legs around him. My dress rucks up around my hips. If any of his neighbors are close enough to see us, they're getting a good look at my panties right now. I can't find it in myself to care as I wrap around him and get lost. His kisses are potent, deadly. I want more.

No. I don't want more. I want *everything*.

"Make love to me, Kane," I demand, writhing against his body, too turned on to care if anyone hears me. Too turned on to care about anything but the ache between my thighs and the heat of his body against mine. I can be Miss Maya, respectable fourth-grade teacher, again tomorrow. For tonight, I'm his. Kane's. And there is nothing respectable about the things I want him to do to me in the cover of darkness. Nothing respectable at all.

# Chapter Five
## KANE

I don't know how we make it from the driveway to my bedroom. Maya is a wild thing in my arms, entirely too tempting. I kiss her again and again, getting lost between those pouty lips and her sweet taste. She's sugar and spice and everything nice. At least while I'm kissing her. As soon as I stop, she turns into a grumpy little kitten.

I'm not sure which I like most. The purring woman in my arms, or the little hellcat who pulls my hair and bites me when I don't give her what she wants quick enough to suit her. By the time I set her on her feet at the foot of my bed, I know one thing for damn sure. There's no turning back now. When I pop that cherry, she's mine.

There's no rule I won't break to keep her. No line I won't cross to make her mine.

Sooner or later, I'll tell her everything, and pray to any God that'll listen that she doesn't kick my ass to the curb. It won't do her any good. I'll set up camp outside her front door until she lets me in if that's what I have to do. But she's mine and I won't give her up.

Fuck what Vanderbilt has to say. They can take my job if they really want it. I don't need it. What I need is this woman naked and writhing on my cock. As soon as humanly possible. For as long as humanly possible.

But I don't rip at her clothes like an untamed beast, even though that's exactly what I want to do. I undress her slowly, taking my sweet time with her. She's the best gift I've ever unwrapped. Every voluptuous inch of skin I unveil is as silky smooth as the last. She's gorgeous, as beautiful half nude as she is fully clothed. More so.

Her eyes are on fire, her creamy skin flushed with desire.

The faint scent of her arousal makes my mouth water. I can't wait to taste it on my tongue.

She groans low in her throat when I tug her dress down and reach out to stroke her full breasts through the pale pink fabric of her bra. I find a hard nipple and pinch.

Her eyes fall closed on a quiet moan.

"You're beautiful," I murmur, my voice gritty. Every soft dip and generous swell on her body is God-given. Not implanted, tucked, or surgically enhanced, but subtly flawed and still flawlessly perfect. Every roll and dimple makes my cock weep for relief. In this town, women pay thousands to erase away every bit of softness they possess. Not Maya. She wears her curves with pride.

"Oh God," she whispers when I roll her nipple between my fingers. As if he stands a chance of stopping me now.

"Come here."

She steps toward me without question.

"Right here," I murmur, turning her with one hand on her hip until she leans into me, snuggled up against my chest. She fits there so well...I ache to keep her. God, how I ache for this woman.

I twine her hair around my fist, lifting the dark mass from her neck.

Dipping my head, I brush my mouth over the soft skin of her shoulder, sliding the straps of her bra down one arm and then the other. Hot, open-mouthed kisses follow the path those little straps of fabric take.

Her head settles against my shoulder, granting me access to the little peaks and valleys of her collarbones. I accept the invitation to those sweet places without hesitation, trailing my tongue and teeth across her exposed skin, familiarizing myself with every sensitive place she offers up to me.

She mewls her approval, her eyes closed.

When I can take no more of her sweet skin against my tongue, I turn her, smiling at the greedy desire etched across her face.

"So fucking perfect," I tell her, putting my hands around her waist and walking her toward the bed.

She smiles again, the bed striking the back of her knees. "So are you."

I groan at her soft answer, loving the honest way she speaks to me. There's no hidden agenda in her compliment. She tells me what she sees in front of her, nothing more nor less. That's rare in my world. With lawyers, there's always an agenda, a reason, or some sort of manipulation behind every compliment or utterance of praise. Some expectation of favor. With Maya, there's none of that. She asks me for nothing, expects nothing, and takes only what I give her of my own free will.

I push her gently back onto the bed and follow her down, nudging her legs apart with my knees. She moans when I hook my fingers into the sides of her panties.

Her back arches off the bed.

I chuckle at her eagerness and lift her hips, sliding the deep green scrap of lace down. She's no shy, timid virgin here. In my arms, she's all woman, trembling and eager. My eyes are trained on her the entire time I strip off her panties, watching as the dark fabric slips down her pale legs. Removing her boots, I fling the tiny piece of fabric away.

"Christ," I say, devouring the way she's spread across the dark sheets like an erotic goddess. She's pink everywhere, with the prettiest little cunt I've ever seen. "Look at you, lamb."

"Kane," she mouths.

I crawl between her legs and drop down over her. I wait until her lips part before leaning down to kiss her again. I could spend an eternity existing off the taste of her lips and not regret a second of it. She kisses me eagerly, her body undulating beneath me as my tongue sweeps inside to steal her breath. One hand trails languidly down her body, my fingertips memorizing every soft curve on their way down. There isn't a single spot on her that I don't want to worship.

Her legs fall open when my palm slides against her hip, teasing. I pause there, tormenting us both, before continuing on to where I'm dying to go. The little taste I got in the parking garage wasn't nearly enough to satisfy me. Wet heat burns against my fingertips as I explore heaven.

I spread her open, rubbing my thumb against her swollen clit.

Her hips jerk toward my touch, her body eager for more. She's so damn responsive. I hope like hell she comes as easily as she did in the parking garage. I want to wring her out, give her as much pleasure as she can stand. Before the night ends, I want her addicted to me. And I don't intend to play fair to make it happen.

"Please," she whispers, rocking against my hand.

"Please what? Tell me what you need, Maya."

I know what she needs. I feel it on levels I can't even begin to describe, but I want to hear her say the words. I need to hear her invite me to touch, to taste...to take.

"Stop teasing me," she groans, writhing beneath me. "Please, Kane. I need you inside of me."

I chuckle at her impatient answer and lift my eyes, my cock pressing twitching at the hungry look on her face. "I will be inside you," I promise, pressing my finger against her little fuckhole. She's so tight I fight to get that single digit inside of her. "But not yet. I want to taste you on my tongue first, lamb."

"Oh!" Her body arches off the bed when I slip another finger inside to join the first.

"Do you want me to eat you?" I ask, pumping and twisting my fingers torturously slow inside of her. There's no chance of loosening her up enough to make taking me easy. But I can make it good for her anyway.

She bobs her head against the pillows, her bottom lip between her teeth.

I hum my approval, memorizing every shift of expression and every twitch of her body as I work her with my hand. She feels like heaven on my fingers. Priceless, pliable. The impatient, greedy beast inside screams to be let out, to be let *in*, but I hold off, wanting to prolong this moment, wanting to savor the way my heart races every time she moans my name.

I prowl slowly down her body, trailing kisses across her creamy flesh as I go. One day soon, I plan to cover those gorgeous tits in my cum. The rest of her too. She'll wear me so anyone who gets too close smells me on her and knows she's taken. There's nothing civilized about that desire. It's purely selfish. But that's okay since I plan to be a selfish, possessive bastard when it comes to her.

Her legs fall open wider on either side of me, as if inviting me in.

My gaze falls on her bare, slick center. Another twist of pleasure stabs deep at the sight of her pink folds and unmistakable need. She's dripping wet for me. I bet I'll be able to taste the cherry in her.

I slide between her legs to find out, lifting her toward my mouth.

My breath washes across her pussy, pulling a groan from her. I groan too, her delicious scent invading every sense until I feel full of her. Spreading her open gently, I revel in the feel of her sticky cream coating my fingers. Of the way she exposes herself to me willingly, letting me take what I want without shame or hesitation.

I dip my head again, blowing across her heated skin.

One swipe of my tongue has both of us moaning—her in pleasure, me from the erotic explosion of her taste against my lips. It warms me, heating me like metal in a forge.

I know only one way to quench the burning thirst.

I set to work on her. Thick honey flows across my lips, trickling down my throat. I hum against her pussy and press my tongue to her clit before jiggling it quickly back and forth.

"Oh God," she cries out, burying her hands into my hair to hold my face to her.

I smile at her response, holding her legs open as I thrust my tongue inside of her. Every time I retreat to tease at her clit, her stomach clenches. The feel of her muscles contracting beneath me adds to the symphony playing across my senses, making me crazy.

My name falls from her lips again and again, a prayerful litany that urges me on as I lick, nip, and suck at her, gorging myself on every response she gives me. I'm an artist with my tongue, hitting just the right spot at just the right time, each long lick and teasing kiss designed to drive her higher.

Her body begins to tremble beneath me, her muscles locking tight as an orgasm comes barreling toward her. God yeah, she's quick to go over. The way she gives herself over to the pleasure is the sexiest thing I've ever seen in my life.

"Kane," she cries, her hands clenched tightly in my hair. "Don't stop. Oh, please, don't stop!"

I don't stop, couldn't stop even if I wanted to. I'm fucking dying to taste her coming on my tongue, to watch her face as the pleasure takes her.

"Come for me, lamb," I breathe against her skin, swiping my tongue across her clit one more time before giving her what she needs. I press my fingers inside of her and curl them up, sucking hard on her clit at the same time.

Her orgasm hits her like a bomb blast, lifting her body up from the bed as wave after wave of ecstasy tears through her. I grab her hips and drive them back down onto the bed, ruthlessly refusing to allow her to escape from what I'm doing to her. I want her to feel every second of pleasure.

Her pussy convulses around my fingers, her body thrashing beneath me. She wails my name into the room.

And I'm fucking dying to get inside of her. I can't hold off any longer. I don't *want* to hold off any longer. As the waves of her orgasm began to subside, I lift my head and look up at her, taking in the euphoric expression on her face.

Christ, she's stunning.

"I need you," I say, rising from the bed to strip off my clothes. My eyes never leave her body as I jerk my shirt off, exposing myself to her. My body is far from perfect. I'm not ripped. I don't have a six-pack. I'm just thick everywhere, muscles hewn from the painstaking, backbreaking work of restoring Ma's house to its former glory.

I don't have to ask to know she likes what she sees.

"Beautiful," she whispers, spreading her legs wider in invitation when I pop the button on my pants. Her gaze roves over my body, shameless in her exploration. Her eyes catch on the tattoo across my ribcage, the one only Kenna has ever seen. She has the same one. We got them right after our dad died. Roses for Ma. Thorns for him. He always said he was a prickly bastard because he had something soft and beautiful to protect.

Maya gives me a soft smile as if she knows exactly what the tattoo represents.

The rest of my clothes fall to the floor and are kicked away. I crawl back up to her, covering her body with mine before my mouth descends on hers again. I know she tastes herself on me, but she doesn't complain. She simply moans my name.

"Are you sure?" I ask, pulling back to stare down into the green eyes that captivate me so completely I can't think straight. But the choice is hers. What she wants, what she needs...nothing else matters.

"Yes," she whispers, no hint of hesitation or doubt.

"I'll make it good for you," I promise. No matter how frantic I am to feast on her body until the ache for her subsides, I'll make it good for her. I want her to remember her first time and burn for more.

I drag her down the bed, spreading her out right where I want her. If I were a gentleman, I'd ask her if she wants me to wear a condom. But I'm not a gentleman, not when it comes to her. I'm a selfish, greedy motherfucker. I want this woman pregnant with my child. I want her tied to me in ways that can't ever be severed. Whoever said love was patient and kind lied. It's wild and untamed and runs purely on base instinct.

"This is going to hurt, sweet lamb," I murmur, trying to prepare her. Even though she's soaked with desire and moaning, there's no way to make this any easier for her. She's smart enough to know that. "Hold onto me."

She wraps her arms around my neck, pulling me down for a kiss. In this moment, she's a brave little soldier, stronger than any man could ever hope to be. That's the thing most men don't get about women. They're stronger than us in every way that counts. They're unflinching in the face of pain, unyielding in the face of fear.

We protect them, not because they're incapable of doing it themselves, but because they're the greatest treasure this world has to offer. I intend to guard this one with my life. This is the only pain she'll ever feel at my hand. For the rest of her life, it'll be only pleasure. More than she can stand.

I line my cock up with her, not even breathing as those first licks of pleasure wash over me. It's gentle rain, warm relief...and the driving need to fuck and claim until I'm sated.

I thrust forward, impaling her on my cock in one powerful thrust.

She cries out as her hymen tears, my name ringing through the room.

I fight like hell to stay still and give her time to adjust as she goes rigid beneath me, squirming in pain. Every little move she makes squeezes my cock in a vise until I'm writhing right alongside her, lost in pleasure while she's lost in pain. I've never felt like a bigger asshole than I do when she whimpers my name.

"I know, lamb," I whisper, pressing my forehead to hers. "You're doing so good. Just stay still for a minute. The pain will stop soon." Christ, I hope it stops soon. Otherwise, I'm going to start ripping shit apart. The fact that she's in pain is killing me. I fucking hate it.

I rain kisses across her face, a litany of apologies spilling from my lips. The last thing I want to do is hurt this extraordinary woman. In a matter of hours, she's become necessary for my survival, an integral part of me. Until three days ago, I didn't believe in love at first sight. I wasn't even sure I believed in soulmates or any of that shit either. Aside from my parents, most married couples I know have gone down in flames.

I've changed my mind. *Maya* changed my mind. If ever there was someone out there designed specifically for me, it's the woman currently in my arms. The one who lights up the room when she smiles and laughs like an angel. She was meant to be mine. I know it with a sense of certainty I've never felt until now, until tonight. Until she walked into Rucker's and the rest of the world ceased to exist.

Does it make me an asshole to admit I don't regret lying to get us here? If so, I'll wear that title proudly. Because this right here could never be wrong. Loving her could never be anything less than perfectly right.

"Kane," she sobs, clawing down my back.

Only then do I realize it's not pain driving her. It's pleasure. She's writhing in ecstasy beneath me, completely undone. Goddamn, she's perfect. And getting more so by the second.

"You feel s-so good," she says, her head tilted back, her hands running all over me. "God, you're so big. I feel like I can feel you everywhere."

What little self-control I had snaps clean in half.

I groan her name and ease almost completely out of her before driving inside again. Her legs wrap around my waist. She takes everything I give her, her nails in my back urging me on. Every hard thrust brings another cry of wonder from her lips.

I savor the feel of her wrapped around me. Of hot heat, soft skin, and raging desire. I want more, more, always more from her. Everything she has to give me.

"Maya, fuck," I groan, sliding almost completely out before thrusting back inside. "You're tight. So fucking tight." I reach down with one hand and flick my thumb across her clit, watching as her body jerks at the sensation, sucking me in even deeper.

"Tell me what you need," I whisper, rubbing my thumb back and forth across her clit as I pump my cock inside her in a deep, even rhythm. "Tell me how you want it."

"Harder," she moans without hesitation.

A growl rips from my throat, echoing in the corners of the room.

I give her what she wants, lifting her hips higher with one hand and slamming myself inside of her, hard and fast. She cries out, lifting her hips again and again to meet my thrusts.

Coherent thought skitters away, leaving behind nothing but what I've wanted since the moment I heard her three days ago. Her skin against mine. That soft voice ringing in my ears. Her tight cunt wrapped around my cock.

"More, more," she chants in soft, throaty moans, her body accepting everything I give her readily, eagerly. She's a siren beneath me, around me, matching my movements thrust for thrust.

I grab her around the waist, flipping her over and lifting her ass into the air. Before she can even miss the feel of my cock sliding deep inside of her, I'm inside her again. Grasping her hips with my hands, I hold her still beneath me, answering her pleas for more.

My hips slap against her in an uncontrolled frenzy. Cries of pleasure—hers and mine—bounce around the room as I let go, let the beast inside take over...and fuck her exactly like I promised. It's fire and ice, pleasure and pain at once. She's so fucking tight it hurts and doesn't hurt enough.

I tangle my hand up in her curly hair, tipping her head back to claim her lips while I fuck her from behind. She writhes and moans, rocking back to meet every hard thrust. Words fall from my lips, words I don't even mean to speak. I give them to her anyway, unable to hold them back when she feels this fucking good wrapped around my cock.

I'm a little pissed I didn't know she existed before three days ago. Had I known she was out there, I would have haunted this city like a fucking wraith until I found her.

"You never should have let me inside this cunt, Maya," I growl, biting her bottom lip. "I'm going to wreck it."

"Do it," she moans, rocking back and forth on her hands and knees, taking me deeper each time. The arch in her back and the way her round ass jiggles drives me insane.

I bite her again, pulling her up onto her knees until her head rests against my shoulder. I run my mouth across her shoulder, nipping, licking, and biting as I fuck her senseless. It's too much for her first time, and yet she doesn't try to stop me. She urges me on, demanding more.

My breath is a jagged, burning pant in my chest, in my throat. Her hair is a binding rope around my hand. Still, I want more.

I tilt her head back further and bite the side of her neck, scraping my teeth along the tendons and pulling a cry from her lips. I splay my other hand across her stomach and inch lower until I bury my fingers in her pussy again, rubbing her clit with the palm of my hand, feeling my cock bump against my fingers with every deep thrust.

The sight of my darker skin against her pale stomach rips through me, obliterating everything but the way she feels around me. I work her furiously. Fucking her, playing with her. Tugging at her hair and biting her neck as the beast inside roars in triumph.

"More, more, more," she pants in harmony with that rabid, primal part of me, her breath coming in gasps.

"I'll give you more," I whisper in her ear. "I'll give you everything, lamb." Everything I have is hers for the taking anyway. Whatever she wants, whatever she needs, I'll find a way to give it to her. She's mine to protect now. Mine to love.

She cries out at my promise, her body clenching around me as I drive her toward completion. And that response—the way she feels coiled tightly around me like she fits me perfectly—drives me on, too.

Everything slows for a moment, each sob of pleasure from her lips lingering in the air longer than the last. Blood pumps through my veins in increments. The heat crackling around us presses in closer, as if we're the only people in the world. I commit each feeling to memory, storing them for the times when I don't have her on her knees just like this. Those long, intolerable hours when the world outside these four walls demands attention.

My name falls from her lips as she explodes around me, her muscles clamping down tight on my cock as she comes in a rush.

I roar her name, my mouth at her ear as I hold her tightly against me, supporting her. Sound, sight...fucking *everything* disappears in an intense rush of pleasure that momentarily stops my heart. I groan my way through it, my balls aching as seed shoots up my cock and into her. It goes on forever, leaving us both writhing, both moaning.

"Kane," she moans, panting for breath as my seed drips from her body. She's a sweaty, sated mess in my arms, practically purring her satisfaction.

We fall to the bed together, wrapped around each other. Somehow, my hand is still tangled up in her hair. She giggles when I try to free it, which has my dick stirring back to life before he's even had a chance to go soft.

"Jesus, baby girl," I growl, pulling her on top of me. I suck in a deep breath and then another, trying to calm the frantic beating of my heart. Blood still rushes in my ears in a torrent of sound. I can't feel my toes. "You keep letting me fuck you like that, and I'm not going to make it to forty."

She cuddles up against me with a soft sigh, not saying anything.

"You okay?" I ask, worried I was too rough with her.

"Mm," she says.

"I need to hear your voice, baby girl," I murmur, brushing strands of hair out of her face. "Did I hurt you?"

"No," she whispers, those pretty green eyes fluttering open. "You didn't hurt me, Kane. You were perfect." A sweet smile lights her up from the inside out, stealing my breath all over again.

"Jesus," I whisper, staring at her in awe. "Where have you been my entire life?"

"Waiting for you."

The way she says it, I almost believe her.

"Not anymore," I vow, rolling until she's on her back beneath me. I lean down to claim her lips, eager to taste her on my tongue all over again. "You're mine now, sweet lamb."

"Yay for me," she whispers back.

# CHAPTER SIX
## MAYA

"*Pride and Prejudice* is not your favorite book," I say, splashing water in Kane's direction. He's lounging at the opposite end of his ridiculously large bathtub, his arms thrown over the sides like an indolent king. He looks edible with a cocky smirk on his face and bubbles sliding down his chest.

We've been in here so long the water is turning my fingers and toes pruney, but neither of us is in a hurry to get out. He was worried he was too rough with me, but I loved every second of being with him. He's bossy though. I wanted to do it again, but he smacked me on the ass and demanded I soak in the tub for a little while.

It didn't take much work to convince him to get in with me. We've been talking for the last hour and a half about everything under the sun. His favorite color is silver, he hates police procedurals but loves Dr. Who. He wanted to be an astronaut when he grew up. His sister is fifteen years younger than he is, but they're the best of friends. He's allergic to cats, hates snakes, but thinks spiders are useful. In short, he's perfectly insane and insanely perfect.

"You're right," he says, grinning at me. "It's not my favorite. I preferred *Emma*."

I roll my eyes at him, convinced he's just teasing me since I confessed how much I love Jane Austen. I've read her entire catalog more times than I care to admit to this crazy man. I love that he knows her books though. Most men turn their noses up at Jane Austen. Not Kane. He's actually read most of them.

"I'm serious, lamb," he says. "Emma is a spoiled society brat who believes that some people are simply better than others because of their station in life. But she learns that where society places you has little to do with your worth and character. People are people, regardless of what family they're born into."

I gape at him, caught off-guard by his summary. It's correct on all points.

"It's the same nature vs nurture discussion we've been having for years," he says, reaching for my foot. He digs his fingers into the arch, making me moan quietly. "Austen challenged a lot of preconceived notions with *Emma*."

"What do you think?" I ask, genuinely curious where he falls in the debate. "Are some people born bad?"

"No," he says. "I think we're all born selfish and self-serving and hedonistic. It's who we are at our core. We're shaped by a lot of shit along the way, but we're all born with the same biological imperatives, the same overarching need to look out for ourselves. Some people learn to overcome those base instincts and do better. They adapt to society. Others suck no matter what life throws at them."

"Kane Maxwell," I say, gaping at him. "You're a cynic."

"I'm a realist," he disagrees. "Taking care of number one is human nature, lamb. Some of us may be civilized and play by a set of agreed-upon rules, but that base instinct still exists in all of us. Most people never get past that. They do what they think is necessary to protect themselves, regardless of who it hurts along the way." He looks me up and down, his expression somber. "You're different. There isn't a selfish bone in your body, sweet Maya."

Guilt whispers through me when I hear the softness in his voice, the pride. I did something selfish tonight, didn't I? I slept with him without him knowing the truth. I wanted him and I took him, even knowing it was wrong. That's the height of selfishness, isn't it? If he's right and people do horrible things because it's human nature to protect themselves, at least they have an excuse. I don't.

"What's that look?" he asks, frowning at me.

"Nothing," I say, slipping my foot from his hands.

*Liar*, a little voice whispers.

Another screams for me to tell him the truth. Except...I really am selfish. Because I don't want him to look at me differently. I want to be the perfect, selfless woman he sees when he looks at me. At least for a little while longer.

"Tell me," he demands, reaching for me again. He wraps a hand around my calf and then reaches for the other. Within seconds, he's hauling me across the tub toward him, completely implacable. Water sloshes over the sides of the tub, but that doesn't deter him.

When I'm on his lap, his hands on my ass, he frowns at me again. "Whatever you're thinking about stole your smile, baby girl. I want to know what it was."

He's not going to let me off the hook. I see the stubborn glint in his eye, the one that attracted me that first day. He stood out from the crowd, not because he was so much bigger than everyone else around him, but because he was so much *more* than everyone around him. He knew he was and didn't make apologies for it. He was comfortable in his own skin, perfectly at ease with his flaws. That was so damn attractive to me. It still is.

"I just...what if I'm not the person you think I am, Kane?" I whisper. "What if I am horrible and selfish? What if I did something...*bad*?"

He eyes me for a moment. "Did you hurt someone, lamb?"

"Maybe," I whisper and then bite my bottom lip when tears fill my eyes. "I didn't mean to do it, Kane. I just wanted to know what it was like."

"Know what what was like?"

This is it. The moment I tell him the truth and he breaks my heart into tiny pieces. And I don't want to know what that feels like. I don't want to watch those obsidian eyes harden and feel him push me away. But I don't want to lie to him either.

I'm so ridiculously in love with him, and every minute I spend with him just tips me a little further over the edge. He's been so good to me because *he's* good. He's a genuinely amazing man. Even if he hates me for it, he *deserves* the truth. I owe him that much.

"What it was like to be yours," I whisper.

His brows pull together, confusion entering his eyes.

"I saw you on campus last semester," I say, rushing to get it out before I lose the nerve to tell him the truth at all. He's so wrong about me. I'm not strong or courageous or selfless at all. I've always been a little bit of a coward, hiding behind school and work and my mom's illness. I lost myself when she died because I never knew who I was to begin with. "You were so damn beautiful to me. I talked myself into approaching you a thousand times, but I didn't want you to know...."

"Know what, Maya?" he growls.

"That I'm not like you!" I cry, throwing my hands up. Bubbles and droplets of water fly all over the place. "You're so damn sexy and smart and fierce. You know who you are and you're comfortable with that. But I've never been that way, Kane. My mom got sick when I was thirteen. All I ever knew was taking care of her. When I lost her, I felt like I lost *me*. I didn't know how to find myself again. I didn't know who I was to begin with. So, when she died, I shut out the entire world and just wallowed."

"You were grieving, lamb," he says, his voice soft. "There's no right way to do that."

"I know," I whisper. "But I crumbled and then I didn't know how to pick myself back up again. Last spring, my best friends finally dragged me out of the house. They told me I couldn't stop living just because my mom died, and that I had to figure out who I was without her. I knew they were right, so I started going to classes again. I started trying to *live* again. And then I saw you and I just...I wanted to meet you so bad."

"Why didn't you introduce yourself, Maya?"

"Because you *weren't* a mess," I mutter. "You had life all figured out, but I was just stumbling through every day, trying to figure out where I fit in the world. It seems silly, but I convinced myself that you'd look right through me if I approached you."

"Maya," he says, a gentle reproach in his tone.

"I wanted you to like me, Kane," I whisper. "But how could you when I didn't even know who I was? I had to figure that out first, but I couldn't stop thinking about you. So, I did something selfish and horrible."

"What did you do, lamb?"

"I lied to you," I whisper. Even if I didn't lie outright, I lied by omission. I'm pretty sure one is just as bad as the other, so I don't try to equivocate or rationalize it. "I'm not just a random grad student. Come Monday, you'll be my educational law professor, Kane."

His eyes widen in genuine shock, confirming what I already knew. He didn't know.

"I knew it when you matched me," I whisper, hanging my head. I've never felt smaller than I do right now. "But I wanted you so damn bad and I just took what I wanted without even considering how it would make you feel. So see? You're wrong about me. I'm selfish too."

He's completely silent.

"I'm so sorry, Kane," I say, trying not to cry even though tears are already slipping down my cheeks. "I've been in love with you for so damn long. I was desperate. It's not an excuse. Of course it's not. There isn't one. I just...I just wanted you, and I knew if I told you the truth, you'd change your mind."

"Maya."

"I'm so, so sorry."

"Maya."

"You should know I decided to drop the class before I slept with you," I say, sliding off his lap. Trying to, anyway.

He refuses to cooperate. He wraps his arms around me, holding on when I struggle to free myself. And that just makes me cry harder. He's being so gentle even though I don't deserve it.

Why didn't I just tell him the truth from the beginning?

How am I supposed to teach tiny humans about honesty and character and integrity when my own is in shambles at my feet? I don't know. But I've never been more disappointed in myself than I am right now. My whole life, I tried to do the right thing. But the one time it really counts, I do the exact opposite.

Even if he's right and we are born selfish and self-serving, we're supposed to learn better. We're supposed to *be* better. But I wasn't. When it comes to him, I'm weak and selfish. And even though I know it's wrong, I think I feel bad *because* I don't feel bad. I got to meet him. I got to hold him in my arms. I got to know what it's like to be his. And that feels so damn amazing to me. I never wanted to hurt him. I just wanted to be his. So bad.

God, I want this man like I've never wanted anything.

"Stop fighting me, beautiful girl," he growls.

"Then let me go," I whisper.

"No."

I know he means it. He's not going to let me go.

I drop my head forward, the fight draining out of me. He hauls me up against his chest and then stands. Water sluices off us in a flood. It doesn't slow him down any at all. He steps out of the tub, holding me tightly. A second later, a fluffy towel flutters down around me.

He doesn't even stop to dry us. He just covers me up and then marches out of the bathroom and back into his bedroom. Like him, it's beautiful. Everything is dark and masculine and sturdy. Fluffy white rugs cover the original hardwood floors. He lives in paradise, painstakingly pre-serving his childhood home just because he didn't want his mom to regret giving it up.

No, I'm not like him. There's no one else in this whole world like him. He's everything I imagined he would be and so much more. I loved him before I knew him, but I fell in love with him tonight. Like a comet crashing to earth. And when he leaves, the crater he's going to leave behind will be massive.

I land on the bed on my back. He doesn't give me time to move before he's on top of me, straddling my hips. He doesn't let me avoid his gaze either. One rough hand gently turns my head, forcing me to face him.

"You said you're in love with me," he says.

"I..." I open my mouth and then close it several times. There's no squirming out of this though, so I don't even try. I'm not sure I even want to try. If this is the part where he tells me that he'll never feel the same, at least this once, I'll have told him how I feel. He doesn't have to love me back for me to be grateful I got the chance to love him even for a little bit. Because in loving him, I figured out who I want to be in life.

I want to be the woman he saw when he looked at me. I want to be the brave girl who takes a chance and doesn't care if the whole world is watching. I want to be the one who loves with her whole heart and soul and doesn't hide from life. I want to be *his*. But if I can't be that, if I ruined my one chance...I want to be honest.

"Yes," I whisper. "I know you probably don't feel the same, especially right now. I don't blame you. But I'm in love with you, Kane. I have been for a long time."

"How long, Maya?"

"Since I saw you the first time," I admit. Even though it sounds crazy, it's true. I loved him the second I set eyes on him. Watching him for the last few months only made that feeling grow. Being with him tonight cemented it. I'm wildly in love with this man. "I know that doesn't excuse what I did. I should have been honest with you."

"You should have," he agrees. "It would have saved you a lot of unnecessary guilt, lamb."

"I'm sorry. I..." I realize then what he said and blink at him. "What?"

"You aren't a bad person." He narrows his eyes on me, disapproval stamped across every line of his face. Somehow, he's even gorgeous when he's grumpy. "You keep thinking you are, it's going to piss me off."

"I lied to you. I...I took advantage of you."

A sharp burst of laughter escapes his pursed lips. "I'm pretty sure I was a willing participant in everything we did tonight," he says. "And I damn sure wasn't complaining."

"You didn't know you were my professor then," I remind him.

"You're right," he says, and then blows out a sharp breath. "But you're assuming that would have changed things for me. You'd be wrong, Maya." He brushes wet tendrils of hair away from my face. "I still would have been fucking you from behind while you begged for more, lamb."

"Kane," I whisper. How he manages to shock me and turn me on at the same time, I don't know. He says the dirtiest things so casually, as if he's commenting on the weather instead of talking about us having sex. It's way sexier to me than it probably should be.

"If you're bad for not telling me the truth, then I'm going to hell too," he says.

"You didn't do anything wrong."

He cocks a brow at me. "Three days ago, you went to dinner with Cassidy and Megan," he says, his voice soft. "You sat in a booth near the back of the restaurant. You guys drank beer and shared an order of chips and queso. You commiserated over the fact that men on the internet suck."

"How do you know that?" I ask, gaping at him.

"Because I was on the other side of the wall," he says. "I listened to your conversation, Maya. I heard you talking about the app." He swallows hard. "I intended to ask you out, but Ma called. By the time I got her off the phone, you were gone."

"Kane..." I stop to lick my lips. My mouth is completely dry. I'm pretty sure that's because my heart is lodged in my throat, stopping the flow of moisture. "What are you saying?"

"I'm saying I fell in love with that sweet voice and your wicked sense of humor," he says. "I'm saying the thought of you dating some motherfucker on the app pissed me off. I'm saying I joined specifically to match with *you*, Maya."

"You're serious."

He nods. "I knew you were a grad student when I did it. I didn't give a fuck."

"Kane," I whisper.

"So if you're bad, so am I, baby girl," he says, reaching for my hands. He links them with his, pinning them to the bed over my head. "Except there's one difference between us, Maya." He leans down over me, caging me in beneath him.

I feel his chest hair against my nipples. Feel his heat seeping into me. I get a little lost again, in him this time. Somehow, this isn't unfolding at all like I thought it would. I expected him to be furious. But judging by the way his erection lays heavy against my belly, he isn't mad. Not even close.

"What difference?" I gasp, writhing beneath him.

"I don't regret a goddamn thing," he growls in my ear before sinking his teeth into my lobe.

I cry out his name, hope bursting in my heart. I feel like I ate a pack of Poprocks again, only this time, the feeling isn't isolated to my stomach. Every part of me pops and fizzes as hope and desire rush through me in tandem, setting me on fire.

"I'd do it again, Maya," he says. "When it comes to you, I don't give a fuck about the rules or right or wrong. You're mine, and I intend to be completely selfish with you."

"Kane," I whisper, feeling a little like I just got launched from hell straight into heaven. I didn't even have to answer any questions as the pearly gates. St. Peter just threw them open wide and let me waltz right in.

"I'm in love with you," he says. "If I have to resign to keep you, that's what I'll do. But I'm not letting you go. So you need to go ahead and get that thought out of your head right now, lamb. Otherwise, I'll be tying you to this bed until you see things my way."

"I don't want you to let me go," I whisper.

"Good girl," he says and then nuzzles his face into the side of my throat. "Goddamn, Maya. I wish like hell I'd have seen you last semester. You'd already be carrying my kid if I had."

"I was a mess. I still am," I admit.

"That's all right. You can be my mess." He sets the flat of his tongue against the pulse hammering in my throat and then groans, shifting restlessly on top of me. "Are you wet for me yet, sweet Maya? Or do I need to lick you good and proper before I fuck you again?"

"I'm ready," I say. I'm so wet, and it's not from the tub either.

"That's not what I asked, baby girl. I asked if you're wet."

"Yes," I whisper.

"Say the words," he growls in my ear. "Let's see how bad you can be."

Not nearly as bad as him, as it turns out. But I give it my best shot anyway.

"I'm not wet, Kane," I say, running my hands down the muscles in his back. I wrap my legs around his hips, opening myself up to him. "I'm soaked for you."

"Let me feel it."

He still has my hands pinned to the bed, so I tighten my grip and move our arms, maneuvering until I'm able to slide them between our bodies. It takes a little more effort and a lot more courage than I expected but I don't think there's anything this man could ask for that I wouldn't willingly give him. I press our hands to my center, letting him feel for himself how wet I am.

"Fuck," he growls. "Touch your pussy for me, Maya. Play with that sweet cunt."

My cheeks heat, but I give him what he wants, moaning as I touch myself. He keeps his hand over mine the entire time, feeling what I do. His breath grows ragged, choppy. Mine does too. I'm so turned on it's ridiculous.

"How many times did you play with yourself while thinking about me, lamb?"

"A lot," I gasp, writhing beneath my own touch. With him right here, every little jolt of pleasure is more powerful, somehow bigger than usual. It feels so damn good. I never thought of myself as particularly naughty or kinky. But I think I might have a little bit of an exhibitionist kink, because I like knowing he's watching me. I liked it in the parking garage too, the risk of being caught. "It's always you, Kane. When..." I groan when he shifts positions, lining up at my entrance. "When I touch myself, it's always you."

"Then make your fantasies come true, Maya. Make yourself come while I'm inside you," he orders me before thrusting forward.

I throw my head back, moaning as he fills me. It stings a little as he stretches already tender muscles. But that little bite of pain is no match for the powerful current of pleasure that runs in tandem with it. Nothing competes or compares to that.

"Make yourself come," he says, holding himself above me on his forearms. His eyes are locked on where we're joined, tracking every move I make.

With his eyes locked on me, I don't feel embarrassed or ashamed. How can I when I see the savage desire on his face? When I hear it rumbling from his lips? This wicked man and the devil on my shoulder are going to be good friends, I can already tell.

I can't wait. I want to experience everything with him, every way possible.

I touch myself, moaning as I circle my clit. He shifts back onto his haunches and then drags me into his lap. My legs are splayed wide on either side of him, letting him see it all. It doesn't take much to get there. Just knowing he's watching me, just feeling him inside me is enough to have me gasping his name and coming in minutes.

As soon as he feels it, he growls my name and starts to move. He fucks me in shallow thrusts, as if he's unwilling to lose even the smallest bit of my heat. He kneads my cheeks in his palms as he fucks me, lifting and separating them. He smacks one cheek and then the other before thrusting a little deeper, a little harder.

"You're spending the weekend here," he growls. "Right here on my cock like this."

"Yes," I agree, more than willing to give him that. Right here is quickly becoming my favorite place. This is quickly becoming my favorite position. He's in complete control of my body like this. But still, he makes me touch myself. Still, he demands I make myself come for him. As if he's not already going to make me come on his own.

When my muscles lock down on him this time, he growls my name and then flips me onto my stomach. His body comes down over mine, pinning me to the bed again. And then this becomes my favorite position. I'm completely helpless beneath him, unable to move more than an inch or two. But I'm not afraid. It feels too damn good to allow fear to have a place.

I want this man to have control of me. God knows I'm not doing a very good job of being in charge of myself. Except...right here, right now, that doesn't feel like a bad thing. For the first time, I feel like maybe it's okay that I don't have it all figured out just yet. Maybe, just maybe, the journey is the important part, not the end result. It doesn't matter if I'm a mess. I'm allowed to be. It doesn't matter if I have it all figured out yet or not. I'm not on a schedule.

The important thing is that I'm trying. I'm not hiding in my apartment and crying myself to sleep. My mom died and it's horrible. It'll never be okay, and I'll always feel like part of me is missing. But I'm still here. I'm living. That's what she'd want for me. It's what I want for me too. To live. To love. To experience the world and all it has to offer.

Kane fucks me hard, pounding into me in ruthless strikes that rattle the bed beneath me and leave me screaming his name.

"That's it, lamb," he growls, biting my shoulder. "Scream for me. Come for me. Goddamn, Maya. I want to be the reason that sweet voice is hoarse and you're walking bow-legged all semester."

If he keeps it up, he will be. Because nothing has ever felt this good before. I feel him everywhere, as if he's the air around me. I breathe him in and blow him out. Over and over until I'm no longer sure where I end and he begins. Until I'm convinced he's going to fuck his way into my soul. When I come, it'll be in pieces around him. And I'll love every minute of it.

"When they ask why you can't sit still, you can tell them it's because your professor was nine deep all night, Maya," he says in my ear, his voice full of wicked intent.

As soon as he says it, I realize something I didn't before. Something he figured out. It wasn't the thrill of getting caught or of being watched that turned me on earlier. It was the thrill of the forbidden. And God help me, but the fact that he's my professor is a hell of a thrill. It's doing things to me it definitely shouldn't.

"Kane," I whimper, clawing at the bed, a little terrified to give into it.

"It's okay, lamb," he croons in my ear, running a soothing hand down my side. "I won't tell anyone how much you like letting your professor do this to you. It'll be our little secret."

God, he's going to ruin me. I know he is. And I'm not going to lift a finger to stop him. I *want* this man to ruin me for anyone else. I want him to be the only thing I ever see...and I want to be the only one he ever sees too.

There's a reason we both did the things we did to end up here. Maybe they were wrong. Hell, maybe we're wrong for doing them. But I refuse to believe love is wrong. I refuse to believe that *we're* wrong. We aren't. This wicked man was made for me, and I was made for him. The app promised me a soulmate, but mine was already there for the taking. I just had to let myself believe it.

I believe it now. With him inside me, on top of me, whispering sinfully wicked and delightful things in my ear, how can I not? Professor Kane Maxwell is mine. My lover. My soulmate. *Mine.*

"Be a good girl and come all over me, Maya," he says, nipping my shoulder again. "I need to feel you dripping down my balls while I'm getting you pregnant with my kid."

He forces my legs a little wider, tilting my hips up. The change in position allows him to slide deeper, until I feel him rattling my soul with every wicked thrust. I cry out his name, wailing it into the room as I shatter apart in a matter of moments, helpless to do anything but give him exactly what he wants.

He pounds into me without rhythm, roaring my name as he follows me over the edge. His seed warms my belly as thick ropes of it shoot from him and spill into me. He's so deep, I feel the broad head of his cock against my cervix. I'm not sure if it's possible to will myself pregnant, but I give it my best shot. I want this man's babies. I want everything he has. Permanently.

Even then, it won't be enough for me. I'm selfish when it comes to him. But I don't feel bad about it this time. I think maybe love is supposed to make us selfish. How else are we supposed to know it's real?

As he slumps above me, raining kisses and words of praise all over my back and shoulders, I *know* this is real. This is forever.

"Sweet Maya," he whispers, running reverent hands all over me. "I love you, lamb."

"I love you too, Kane. So damn much."

# CHAPTER SEVEN
## KANE

"You can't quit your job!" Maya says, staring at me like I just grew a third head.

"Last I checked, I could do whatever I wanted to do, lamb," I say, prowling across the kitchen toward her. She's perched on the island, wearing nothing but my t-shirt. It looks a lot better on her than it does on me, that's for damn sure. I'm supposed to be cooking her breakfast, but I'd much rather eat her again. The hobbits were onto something with second breakfast.

"Kane, they're counting on you," she says, batting my hands away when I try to get them on her. Being right has never been as satisfying as it is right now. I *can't* keep my hands off her. Don't even want to try. I've been all over her since I brought her home with me on Friday, and it's still not enough. "It makes more sense for me to withdraw from the class."

"You need the seminar to graduate, Maya," I remind her.

"I can take it next semester."

"Hate to break it to you, baby girl, but if they don't want your boyfriend teaching a class with you in it, they damn sure won't like your husband teaching it," I say, tipping her chin up until her eyes meet mine.

Her mouth gapes open, making me smile. She's so fucking cute when she's all flustered and off-balance. It's not hard to fluster her. She's so innocent. I can't wait to spend the rest of my life trying to fuck it out of her. I already know it'll never happen. No matter what filthy shit I say or how many times I get inside her, she'll still turn the sweetest pink and stare at me in awe when I say something she wasn't prepared to hear.

"You want to marry me?"

"Sweet lamb," I croon, shaking my head. "Did you think I'd settle for anything less than my ring on your finger?" I run my hands up her thighs, parting them while she's distracted. Her pink cunt peeps out at me from between her thick thighs. My dick instantly responds, hardening in my boxers. "When I said you were mine, I meant it, Maya. You're mine. My ring on your finger, my cum leaking from this sweet little hole, my kid in your belly *mine*."

"Caveman," she mumbles, moaning when I part her slit with my thumb.

"No, lamb. I won't be dragging you back to the cave by your hair. You won't be lifting a goddamn finger to serve me," I say, pressing gently on her shoulder until she lays back, giving me access to what I want. I pull her t-shirt up over her hips, exposing that juicy cunt. "I'll be the one doing all the work, and I plan to work real hard."

"Kane," she gasps, grasping onto the edge of the countertop when I settle on a stool in front of her and get to work. I eat her like I don't already have her taste in the back of my throat, like I didn't already have her coming all over me before we left the bed this morning. With her, it's never enough. Poor lamb is going to spend the rest of her life sore and dripping my cum. I fully intend to have her bent over and screaming my name at every available opportunity.

If that makes me a caveman, I'm willing to wear that title. But she won't be giving anything up for me. She won't be taking care of me or our house or doing anything she doesn't want to do. Her whole life, she's been taking care of her mom, watching her slowly slip away. She's been through hell and back and she's been through it alone. It's her turn to be taken care of for a little while.

"Oh god, oh god," she cries, writhing as I curl my fingers up and stroke her g-spot while sucking on her hard little clit. Within seconds, she's coming all over me again, crying my name into the kitchen when she does it.

I eat her through it, licking up every drop of honey that flows from her. If I could survive on her, I'd do it without hesitation. Her taste is addictive. So are the sweet sounds she makes and the way those pretty eyes turn glassy and her cheeks flush. She's beautiful all the time, but she's otherworldly when she's coming for me.

When she falls limp beneath me, plastered to the island, I place a soft kiss on her lower belly and then another between her breasts, right over her heart. It races against my lips.

"You're marrying me, lamb," I whisper before claiming her lips in a soft kiss.

She moans into my mouth, her arms coming up to wrap around me. My dick is rock hard and raring to go, but I ignore him, content to cuddle the shit out of her for a while. I never knew how good it could feel to simply hold someone. But she fits in my arms just right.

"I'll marry you," she whispers. "But I want something first."

"You can have whatever you want."

"I want to drop the seminar."

"Except that," I say, frowning. She needs it to graduate. She didn't work as hard as she did for as long as she did just to give it up now.

"Kane." She huffs and then nudges my shoulder to get me off her.

I grumble under my breath but reluctantly peel my body from hers, allowing her to sit up. She's all rumbled and sexy, but I see the determination lurking in her eyes. She's going to fight me on this.

"You have to let me drop it," she says, reaching for my hand. "It's important to me."

"Why?"

"Because it's the right thing to do," she says, tipping her head back to look at me. "Because I learned something about myself this weekend. I'm selfish when it comes to you. But I can't be selfish with you if it's at your expense. I don't like the way that feels at all. I don't want to be that kind of person, Kane."

"Fuck," I growl and then I expel a breath. As much as I don't want her to drop the seminar, I know she's right. If I don't agree to let her drop it, she'll spend the entire semester feeling horribly guilty. I don't want that between us. I don't want her to carry that. She's a gentle little lamb, with a guilty conscience and a strong sense of right and wrong. She felt badly enough about not being honest with me from the start. I won't allow her to feel like what's between us is wrong or fucked up or anything less than the gift it is. If dropping the class makes her feel better, I have to give it to her.

"Fine," I say. "I'll let you drop the seminar instead of resigning. But I want something in return."

I know it's the right decision as soon as I say it. The guilt in her eyes vanishes, snuffed out by the smile overtaking her face. How she could ever think she's anything less than perfect is beyond me. She may not know who she is just yet, but I do, and she's a fucking queen. I can't fucking wait to see her grow into it, can't wait to see who she becomes in fifteen years, in twenty. I already know she's going to own me through every minute of it. Hell, she already does.

"What?" she asks, cocking her head to the side.

"I want you to take me to meet your mom."

She blinks wide eyes at me.

"I want to meet her, lamb," I murmur, running my thumb across her bottom lip. That mouth is quickly becoming an obsession of mine. "I've got a few things to tell her."

"You do?" She smiles at me, looping her arms around my neck. "Like what?"

"Thank you, for starters," I say, tipping my head down to brush my lips across hers. Yeah, I'm obsessed with that mouth. It's damn near as sweet as her cunt. "She brought you into this world. I'd like to thank her for that."

"Kane," she whispers, melting against me.

"I also plan to let her know that I'm marrying you," I say, wrapping one hand around her hip to pull her closer. Breakfast is going to have to wait. I release her long enough to pull my boxers down, not bothering with taking them off. I just tug them down enough to free my cock, and then yank her ass to the edge of the island.

She wraps around me like a blanket, all cuddly and sweet. All warm and wet. Fuck, she's pretty when she's turned on. I thrust into her slowly, taking my sweet time. My eyes threaten to roll back in my head as her wet heat surrounds me. We moan in unison, unraveling together.

"I want her to know that you're going to be okay," I say once she's impaled on my cock. "She should know I'll be watching over you from now on."

"Kane," she whispers, her eyes filling with tears. With awe. I can't wait to give her reasons to keep looking at me that way for the rest of her life. The rest of the world may think I'm a grumpy bastard, but not Maya. In her eyes, I'm a fucking rockstar.

"It's true," I murmur against her lips. "I'm here now. If you cry yourself to sleep, missing your mom, you won't be doing it alone anymore. I'll be here to hold you through it. And when you're done, I'll help you pick up the pieces and put yourself back together again. For as long as it takes for you to know that you're going to be just fine now. And you *are* going to be okay, lamb. Even if I have to hold all your pieces together myself."

"Kane," she sobs into my mouth, making me smile. "I love you so much."

"Sweet, sweet Maya," I whisper, lifting her completely off the island and into my arms where she belongs. Where she'll always belong. No, she's not a mess. She's *my* mess, and I wouldn't have her any other way. "I love you."

# Epilogue
## MAYA

### **Five Years Later**

"Ma, you don't need another house," Kane growls.

Kenna and I share a look, both fighting laughter. I'm pretty sure his mom only brings up buying a new house to stress him out. Anytime he gets too comfortable, she slips it into conversation. His head immediately explodes. It shouldn't be nearly as amusing as it is, but it always makes me and Kenna laugh like crazy.

My husband is good at a lot of things. Keeping his feelings about renovations to himself is not one of them. Even though we finished renovating his mom's place three years ago, he still gets all worked up about it. I'm pretty sure he would have built that time machine and gone back to South Africa circa 100,000 years ago to put the kabosh on the creation of paint if he could have done it.

Kenna and his mom love to tease him about it. He gets so grumpy. But even though he hems and haws and swears he's putting his foot down, I know he'd renovate a thousand houses if it made his mom happy. He dotes on her and Kenna. He dotes on me too. He is so good to all of us. It blows my mind that no one else ever scooped him up because he's one of the most incredible men I've ever met. But I'm glad no one else ever caught his eye.

I don't know what my life would be like without him in it, but I know it would be less. The last five years have been some of the best years of my life. He's my best friend, my lover, a piece of my soul. I'm not lost anymore. I'm not a mess anymore. Okay, I'm still a mess. But Kane taught me that it's okay to be a mess. He taught me that no one really has life all figured out.

We're all just doing the best we can with the cards we've been dealt. Sometimes, we do okay. Other times, we get a little lost and fall apart and forget to get back up again. But the important thing is that we try. We grow. We change. And, if we're really lucky, somewhere along the way, we find the things that really matter in life. Love. Family. Purpose. The rest works itself out eventually.

God knows it has for us. We jumped in with both feet and never looked back. Our life isn't perfect. But it's perfect *for us*. We're perfect *for each other*. Not a day goes by when I'm not grateful for Kane and the incredible life we've built together. Not a day goes by when I don't love him a little bit more than I did the day before. Not a day goes by when I wouldn't choose him over everyone and everything, no questions asked.

He didn't just put me back together, he helped me build something new, something stronger. I still miss my mom every single day. Sometimes, I still cry myself to sleep. But when I'm done, Kane lifts me to my feet and reminds me who I am and what I'm capable of. He reminds me that she's still with me and that I'm going to be okay. He loves me, even when I forget to love myself.

"I will if you keep giving me grandbabies, dear," his mom says, patting him on the cheek as she swishes by him on the way to the sink. She winks at me and Kenna. "I'm running out of room."

Kenna practically chokes on her cookie.

"You have five grandkids," Kane says, his eyes narrowed on his mom. "And I had nothing to do with two of them."

"Actually," I say, squeezing Kenna's hand when she grabs mine under the table. She and her mom already know the news. Kane doesn't. We've been trying for another baby for months now, but this time took a little longer. I was beginning to worry that something was wrong. Right up until I smelled Kenna's coffee this morning and promptly threw up my breakfast.

Kane's mom was so excited. She demanded I take a test right then and there. It was positive. Kane Maxwell is going to be a daddy again. I've been weepy about it all day. He is so good to our girls. He treats them like they're little princesses. In return, they idolize him.

Our oldest, Rosalie, would go to war for her daddy. She's fierce and brave and will probably bring the world to its knees someday. She already wants to be a lawyer and professor just like her daddy. Kylie, our three-year-old, is more like me. She's a bit of a mess. But she's so sweet and affectionate!

Our youngest though...Lord have mercy, our youngest is a handful. She's not even two yet, but she's already a wild child. When something upsets her, the whole world hears her outrage. She's loud and passionate and wildly untamed. I love her so much, and so does Kane. He's the only one who can ever get her to sit quietly for longer than five minutes. The rest of the time, she's causing chaos and mayhem.

"She might need one more room," I say.

Kane whips around to face me so fast I'm surprised he doesn't give himself whiplash. I can tell by the look in his eye that he already knows what I mean. He's too damn smart. Nothing escapes him or slips past him. It's part of what makes him such a good lawyer. But he doesn't steal my thunder. He waits patiently for me to tell him.

"I have something for you," I say.

Kenna reaches under the table and grabs the gift bag for me.

I hold it out to Kane, who prowls across the room in complete silence. Before he takes the bag, he leans down and kisses me. I sigh against his lips, melting a little. I swear, this man kisses like no other. As soon as his lips touch mine, everything else simply ceases to exist. It's been like that for five years. I hope it never changes.

Once he's kissed me into a stupor, making his mom and Kenna laugh, he pulls back, grinning like he's proud of himself. He's always kissing me in front of them. It used to drive me crazy, but I don't even try to get him to stop anymore. He never does. He says I belong to him, and he'll kiss me whenever he damn well pleases. Kenna and his mom don't seem to mind.

Honestly, Kenna's husband is just as bad as Kane! He's always kissing her in front of everyone. Gideon Carmichael makes no secret of the fact that he worships the ground Kenna walks on. He and his brothers own a private security company. He saved her life from her crazy manager right after Kane and I got married. She fell for him so hard. They've been blissfully happy ever since.

All of her dreams have come true. She's a big deal in country music now. She even won album of the year last year. I love seeing all of her work paying off for her. Kenna is the sister I never had. I love her so much!

No one says anything as Kane reaches into the bag and pulls out the shirt wrapped in tissue paper. He gives me a questioning look before he tears into it, but he doesn't ask any questions. He just plays along, letting us have our fun.

As soon as he unwraps it, he flips the shirt out so he can read the front of it.

"This womb is undergoing renovation," he reads aloud.

No one says anything as he slowly lowers the shirt. His obsidian eyes lock on mine, blazing with heat. His gaze doesn't waver as he carefully sets the t-shirt aside and then hooks a foot underneath the leg of my chair. It scrapes across the tile floor as he drags me closer to him.

"Ma?" he says when I'm right in front of him.

"Yes, dear?"

"I love you and Kenna like crazy," he says, still not looking away from me. The heat in his eyes... Lord, I'm in trouble.

My entire body trembles in anticipation.

"I know that, dear," his mom says, amusement in her voice.

"Good. Because I need you and Kenna to leave my house right now," he says.

"Kane!" I cry, burying my face in his stomach to hide my laughter. He's impossible and shameless and ridiculous. And I wouldn't change a single thing about any of it.

"Of course, dear," his mom says, not in the least offended. She and Kenna are laughing too. They're used to him being ridiculous. Thank God. I know it would break his heart if he truly upset one of them being all bossy and highhanded.

He wraps a hand around the back of my neck, holding me against him as his mom and Kenna hug him and say congratulations. They both squeeze my arm and tell me that they love me. Losing my mom was devastating, but I didn't just get Kane when he found me on the dating app. I got a sister and a mom-in-law too. Mary told me once that she would never dream of trying to replace my mom, but that she hoped I'd be okay with letting her love me like one too.

And she has. She treats me like I'm her own daughter. She's a free spirit with a big heart and the craziest ideas. My mom would have loved her. I know I do. She's exactly what I needed to help shrink the hole in my heart. It'll never close entirely, but I'm not alone anymore. I have a family now. They're loud and messy and wild and crazy and I'd fight to the death to protect them. I know they'd fight for me too.

"You're in trouble, lamb," Kane says as soon as they're gone.

"Yay me," I whisper, letting him lift me from the chair into his arms. I wrap my legs around his waist and my arms around his neck, smiling so big my cheeks hurt. "You're going to be a daddy again, Kane."

"Fuck yeah, I am," he growls, his hands on my ass. He spins toward the island before setting me on top of it. "Lay back, lamb. Let me say hi to my baby girl."

I let him help me lay back, tears filling my eyes when he immediately pulls my shirt up and drops his forehead to my belly. He makes the softest sound of contentment against my skin, one that lets me know beyond a shadow a doubt that he's happy.

"Hi, sweet girl," he whispers to our baby. "I helped make you."

"Kane!" I say, laughing.

He lifts his head and grins at me, completely unrepentant. "What?" he says. "It's true."

"I thought you wanted a boy," I say, brushing his dark hair back from his forehead. It's shot through with gray now, but it hasn't slowed him down any at all. I don't think anything ever will. He's as gorgeous as ever, maybe more so. Being a daddy looks good on him.

"Baby girl, I'd fucking love to have a boy to help keep an eye on all my girls," he says. "But the fucking universe is determined to keep me humble by keeping me outnumbered. You're having another perfect little girl, just like the last three."

"You could be wrong," I say, though secretly, I'm pretty sure he's right and this one will be a girl too. I don't think the universe is the one doing it though. His sperm is responsible for that. And they've decided to give my growly man a gaggle of little girls to keep him on his toes. We wouldn't trade him for anything in the world. No one loves us better than Kane.

"Nah," he says, lifting my hips to slide my pants and panties down my legs. "I'm not. The universe is aligned against me. I accepted it when you got pregnant last time, lamb." Once my clothes are gone, he tips his head to my belly again, placing a sweet kiss right below my navel.

"Sweet girl, I need you to go to sleep in there. Daddy is about to do wicked things to your mommy."

"Kane!"

"Our daughter isn't going to listen to me fucking you, Maya," he growls, lifting his head to look at me like I'm the crazy one here. "And since you just told me that you're pregnant again, I will be fucking you, lamb. My dick is going to break off if I don't."

"You're insane, you know that?" I say, shaking my head at him. I'm smiling too. With him, I'm always smiling. He keeps me so damn happy all the time. Part of me wishes like hell that I'd been brave enough to introduce myself the first time I set eyes on him. The rest of me, though? Well, the rest of me thinks things worked out exactly the way they were meant to work out.

I know who I am now. I'm *his*.

"You love me," he says, reaching over his head to grab his shirt. He pulls it off in one fluid motion before dropping it to the floor.

"I do," I whisper, watching as he undresses for me. "I love you so damn much, Kane Maxwell."

"Yeah?" He grins, a wholly wicked grin that I feel deep in my belly as he steps up in front of me again. His dark eyes rove over my body, his fist wrapped around his erection.

His expression is soft, full of pride as he looks me over. "Then I'm the luckiest motherfucker alive, lamb."

"Me too," I whisper. So damn lucky.

He leans down and kisses me softly, lingering against my lips like it's his favorite place to be. Once I'm panting for breath and writhing beneath him, he pulls back, hitting me with a look that's hot enough to set the island beneath me on fire. "Now be a good girl and make yourself come so I can lick it all up, lamb," he growls. "And then I'll give you what you really want."

"W-what do I really want?" I ask, my hand already sliding down my body.

"Another reason to scream my name."

My quiet laughter turns to a moan as he slides his hand over mine, guiding it to my folds. Like always, I'm soaked for him. Aching. Desperate. I'm not the only one though. As we work together to make me come, I know he's just as desperate. In that way, we've always been perfectly matched. He completes me...but I complete him too. Exactly like we were meant to do.

We are soulmates, after all.

# Author's Note

If you enjoyed Learning Curve, please consider leaving a review! They are so helpful for authors.

Model Behavior, the next book in the One Night with You series, is now available!

# MODEL BEHAVIOR

### EXCERPT

"Turn to the left," Sage says. As soon as I move, he sighs. "Left, baby girl. Not right."

"Sorry," I whisper, my face flaming. I quickly move to the left, only to list sideways. Reaching out, I grab the back of the chaise just before I land on my ass in the floor.

"Shit," Sage says, lowering the camera. "Are you okay?"

"Yes," I whisper and then exhale a breath. This has turned into a train wreck. He probably thinks I'm a complete disaster. "I'm sorry."

"Stop apologizing."

"Sor..."

He stalks across the room toward me, a deep groove in his forehead from him frowning so hard. "Am I making you uncomfortable, Trinity?"

"No, I..." I trail off with a shake of my head. "No."

He eyes me for a minute, his lips pursed. "You're nervous. Why?"

"I haven't modeled in a long time," I remind him. "I'm just rusty."

He cocks a brow at me, clearly not buying my excuse. "Bullshit. You could be out of the game for half a century and still be a natural. You move like a dream," he says. "Being alone with me makes you nervous."

"I–"

"I'm just not sure if it's because I make you uncomfortable or if it's because you're attracted to me," he murmurs before I can utter a denial. "If it's the former, I'll get Gabby in here so you're able to relax. I don't want you feeling anxious around me."

I inhale a deep breath, reaching for a little courage. "And if it's the latter?"

"And if it's the latter," he says, squatting down beside the chaise so we're eye level, "I'll tell you that you aren't the only one, we'll finish this shoot, and then I'll ask you out to dinner." He holds up a hand, halting me before I can respond. "But I promised myself to behave during this shoot, so I'm trying like hell to honor that promise."

"Oh," I whisper, disappointment flowing through me. The way he says it makes me think he's done this before. I don't like the way that feels. It's like a thorn stabbing me right through the heart. I've never felt this way before, and I guess I just expected that he hadn't ever felt it before either. But who am I kidding? He's older, gorgeous, and spends his days with some of the most beautiful women on the planet. He's probably been with a million women.

"What's that look?" he demands, reaching out to turn my face toward him. He's scowling, his eyes narrowed like he wants to fight whatever upset me. Which is honestly kind of sweet but only makes me feel like an even bigger dork.

"Nothing," I say, shaking my head. "Nothing. I'm just being crazy. Let's just finish this."

"No."

"No?" I blink at him.

"Not until you tell me what you were just thinking about," he says.

"It was nothing," I say, willing him to believe it.

He holds my gaze, silently commanding me to tell him. I try to resist, really, I do. But it's virtually impossible when he's so close I can smell his intoxicating scent and see the flecks of gold in his eyes. When I feel the heat of his big body calling to me. Everything about him makes me want to obey, just to make him call me a good girl again.

Why is that so sexy to me?

"I am nervous about being alone with you," I blurt out.

It might be my imagination, but for a split second, distress flashes through his expression. And then he blinks it away, his gaze settling on my face. He goes completely still, barely even seeming to breathe. "Why does being along with me make you nervous?"

"I don't want to mess this up," I say, not sure how to explain without sounding like a crazy person. "You're not just a photographer, Sage. You're pretty much the best photographer in the world. I don't want to do something wrong when it could impact my models or my business. I don't want you to think I'm not professional."

His brows furrow, his expression darkening.

Uh oh.

"You think I'd do something to hurt your business?"

"Not exactly..."

"Explain," he growls.

I don't understand how he's even hotter when he's angry. It's really not fair.

"I just..." I huff out a breath and send up a silent prayer that I don't live to regret being honest with him. "I'm ridiculously attracted to you, and you know I was thinking about dirty things outside. Now we're alone and I'm freaking out because there's a bed right behind you and I'm still thinking dirty things about you," I say all at once and then slap a hand over my mouth. "Please don't blackball me."

"Blackball you?" He blinks at me, genuinely shocked. "You think I'm going to be pissed that you're attracted to me, Trinity?"

I bob my head in a nod.

"I'd never do anything to hurt you," he vows, his voice so somber I don't doubt him. His eyes blaze like the sun, that same vow reflecting deep in their depths. "Would you believe I've been worried about roughly the same thing?"

"You have?" I ask, trying to wrap my head around that. He's so...*him*. Gorgeous. Talented. Older. There's no way he's been worried about being alone with me. Except I know he isn't lying. I'd stake my life on the fact that he's being honest with me right now.

"You think I go around making demands to work with certain people often?" he asks, cocking a brow at me.

"I guess I assumed you..." I trail off, not honestly sure if I thought that or not.

He cocks a brow at me. "You think all my models get my dick hard? Or that the thought of getting time alone with them makes me fucking crazy? You're wrong." He reaches out slowly, carefully, as if giving me time to move away from him. I don't though. I stay right where I am. His rough fingers touch the side of my face, turning it toward him. "I don't fuck my models, Trinity."

My stomach sinks, despair bubbling up hard and fast.

"You'll be the first."

*Model Behavior is now available!*

# Instalove Book Club

**The Instalove Book Club is now in session!**

Get the inside scoop from your favorite instalove authors, meet new authors to love, and snag freebies and bonus content from featured authors every month. The Instalove Book Club newsletter goes out once per week!

Join now to get your hands on bonus scenes and brand-new, exclusive content from our first six featured authors.

Join the Club: http://instalovebookclub.com

# FOLLOW NICHOLE

Sign-up for the mailing list to stay up to date on all new releases and for exclusive ARC giveaways from Nichole Rose.

Want to connect with Nichole and other readers? Join Nichole Rose's Book Beauties on Facebook!

amazon.com/Nichole-Rose/e/B0847QHXPJ

facebook.com/AuthorNicholeRose/

instagram.com/AuthorNicholeRose

twitter.com/AuthNicholeRose

bookbub.com/authors/nichole-rose

tiktok.com/@authornicholerose

# MORE BY NICHOLE ROSE

### Her Alpha Series
Her Alpha Daddy Next Door

Her Alpha Boss Undercover

Her Alpha's Secret Baby

Her Alpha Protector

Her Date with an Alpha

Her Alpha: The Complete Series

## Her Bride Series

His Future Bride

His Stolen Bride

His Secret Bride

His Curvy Bride

His Captive Bride

His Blushing Bride

His Bride: The Complete Series


## Claimed Series

Possessing Liberty

Teaching Rowan

Claiming Caroline

Kissing Kennedy

Claimed: The Complete Series


## Love on the Clock Series

Adore You

Hold You

Keep You

Protect You

Love on the Clock: The Complete Series

## The Billionaires' Club
The Billionaire's Big Bold Weakness
The Billionaire's Big Bold Wish
The Billionaire's Big Bold Woman
The Billionaire's Big Bold Wonder

## Playing for Keeps
Cutie Pie
Ice Breaker
Ice Prince
Ice Giant (coming soon)

## The Second Generation
A Blushing Bride for Christmas
Come Undone (currently in Love Always Wins antholo-
gy)

## Silver Spoon MC
The Surgeon

The Heir

The Lawyer

The Prodigy (coming soon)

The Bodyguard (coming soon)

## Echoes of Forever

His Christmas Miracle

Taken by the Hitman

Wicked Saint

## The Ruined Trilogy

Physical Science

Wrecked

## Destination Romance

Romancing the Cowboy

Beach House Beauty

## Standalone Titles

A Touch of Summer

Black Velvet

His Secret Obsession

Dirty Boy

Naughty Little Elf

Devil's Deceit

Wearing Their Pearls (coming soon)

**Easy on Me**

Easy Ride

Easy Surrender

**One Night with You**

Falling Hard

Model Behavior

Learning Curve

Angel Kisses

**writing with Loni Ree as Loni Nichole**

Dillon's Heart (coming soon)

Razor's Flame (coming soon)

Ryker's Reward (coming soon)

Zane's Rebel (coming soon)

# About Nichole Rose

Nichole Rose is a curvy romance author on the west coast. Her books feature headstrong, sassy women and the alpha males who consume them. From grumpy detectives to country boys with attitude to instalove and over-the-top declarations, nothing is off-limits.

Nichole is sure to have a steamy, sweet story just right for everyone. She fully believes the world is ugly enough without trying to fit falling in love into a one-size-fits-all box. When not writing, Nichole enjoys fine wine, cute shoes, and everything supernatural. She is happily married to the love of her life and is a proud mama to the world's most ridiculous fur-babies.

You can learn more about Nichole and her books at her website .

facebook.com/AuthorNicholeRose/

instagram.com/AuthorNicholeRose

twitter.com/AuthNicholeRose

bookbub.com/authors/nichole-rose

tiktok.com/@authornicholerose